WHERE THE
MOUNTAINS
KISS THE SKY

CIANA STONE

iii

DEDICATION

As always, for the love of my life.

Chapter One

Caught up in the view from the window seat in first class, Rylee was startled when the flight attendant leaned in over the empty aisle seat to speak with her. "We'll arrive on time if you have someone meeting you."

"Oh, thank you," Rylee smiled.

"Is this your first time visiting Wyoming?"

"Yes, it is. The view from here is stunning."

"Isn't it? Are you visiting family or on vacation?"

"Starting a new job." Rylee still had a little trouble believing she was moving to Brickton, Wyoming.

"Well, congratulations, I hope you'll be happy."

"Thank you, so do I."

As the flight attendant moved away, Rylee turned her attention back to the window. Her mind moved away from marveling over the sights to what led her to be on this flight.

No Limits Cyber Security Systems Integration, or No Limits, as it was most often referred to, was the second job she'd held since graduate school. They tempted her away from a job with the government with a salary that was like a dream to a young woman with a mountain of student loans. Things were definitely more profitable in the private sector. In the nine years she'd worked for them, she'd not only paid off her loans but also her house.

At thirty-seven, she was debt-free and eager for advancement so that she could save for a bigger home. The small home she'd purchased in Orlando, Florida, where she worked, was okay, but she wanted something in a more upscale community, with perhaps a pool.

Rylee didn't anticipate significant advancement with No Limits, but last year was given control of the team in charge of all the websites, webcams, and live feeds from the big resorts, amusement parks, and some beaches. She loved what she did and worked hard to ensure the systems operated flawlessly, with failsafe backups, generators in case of power failures, and daily diagnostics to ensure no interruptions.

She'd never imagined how successful the company actually was, but during her time with them, she'd watched them grow into a corporation now traded on the American stock exchange and one who'd gained a monopoly in the type of services they offered.

Last week, her boss called her in for a meeting. Since it was unscheduled, she was perplexed why he'd take her away from her work. Not that she questioned him, she simply showed up on time.

Ian Grant, her boss, made a name for himself in the United Kingdom, working for the government on internet security. He married an American and moved to the states, where he went into business with two other men and formed No Limits.

Rylee saw him sitting at his desk on the phone and knocked on the glass of his door. He motioned for her to enter, and she did so but remained just inside the door as he finished his conversation, which only took seconds.

"Rylee, have a seat." He gestured to the seating area on the other side of the room, came around from behind his desk, and sat on one of the big leather wing chairs. She opted for a seat on the sofa adjacent to him.

"You wanted to see me, sir?"

"I did. Do you remember Brent Corsa? He's been heading the team up in Wyoming for the last couple of years."

"Yes, I do. We had a couple of interesting conversations about the importance of developing more vendor-agnostic middleware to act as mediators between software from numerous vendors rather than between two specific applications. He has some compelling and brilliant ideas."

"Had," Ian's smile faded. "Brent was killed in an auto accident yesterday."

"Oh no." Rylee hated hearing that news. Brent was a genuinely nice person with a brilliant mind. "What about his partner, Dennis?"

"In critical condition."

"I'm so sorry."

"We all are, but like it or not, we still have a contract to honor, and the Board met last night to decide what to do. It's been decided. We're sending you to Brickton, Wyoming, to take over for Brent."

"Me?" She was stunned. "But what about–"

"Louis is ready to move up. He's been your second in command for three years, and we believe he's ready to take the reins. You've got two days to get him up to speed. We're booking you on a flight to Brickton on Thursday. You'll meet the team, have the weekend to get settled, and then jump in on Monday."

"But…". She didn't know what to say, her mind was in a whirl. "But what about my house? And I don't have –"

"The company will buy your house for above market value. We can close in under a week. We'll have your belongings put into an environmentally controlled storage unit until you decide what you want to do with everything.

"Alternatively, if you prefer, we'll secure a service to keep the house maintained inside and out until you decide what to do with it. The choice is up to you. Oh, and since your car is a compact and not a new model, we'll buy it from you and have a terrain safe SUV waiting for you in Brickton. We're arranging to purchase you a place to live, and the company will pay for all your living expenses."

"Hold on," Rylee raised a hand. "What does that mean?"

"It means it won't cost you a dime to live there."

"Do I still get paid the same?" She was already calculating how much she could save.

"No."

Her heart sank. It was wonderful to get free housing, but that didn't move her closer to her goal, which was to save and invest wisely enough that she could retire by the time she was fifty. "Oh, well..."

Ian rose and walked back to his desk. He picked up an iPad, did something on it, and then replaced it on the desk. A moment later, her phone pinged. "Open that," he directed.

Rylee opened the messenger app and lost her breath when she read the text. "Are you serious?" She reread it. "Did you mistype? This says–"

"And that's the starting salary. We're also giving you stock options and a bonus based on system performance."

"Oh, my –" she looked up from her phone. "Are you sure? There are people in the company with more seniority and–"

"But not half as good." Ian reclaimed his seat. "We recognize talent, Rylee, as well as loyalty, and you demonstrate both in spades daily. This is our way of rewarding that dedication."

She had to smile. "Well, this is one heck of a reward, but couldn't it have been attached to – oh, I don't know – Hawaii? I mean, what's in Brickton, Wyoming?"

"Only one of the highest concentrations of wealth in the country. Consider this. Why would live streaming from the center of a town with a population of under ten thousand, views of parks and stores, bars, and shops, of Yellowstone and Granite Lake, dude ranches and other things, be important?"

"I don't know."

He leaned back in his chair. "Money. Since the implementation of the system there, tourism in the state has risen nearly fifty percent. Because of that, Yellowstone has been granted an enormous influx of cash, making it the most well-maintained national park in the country. Hunting and fishing licenses cost ten times more.

"And believe it or not, since Brent started the subscription service, the revenue it's generated pays for nearly half of our fees. It is, in a word, a gold mine, and thus the salary package we're offering you is a bargain. We want our best there because what they're doing in Wyoming is being noticed and becoming the benchmark. We're already in talks with groups from Montana, the Dakotas, Iowa, and Nebraska for similar systems. Not to mention Los Angeles, New Orleans, Dallas, and New York."

"Wow," Rylee was shocked. "That's amazing."

"Indeed. Thanks to the work that you and others have done. Your agnostic approach has opened eyes to new ways of making technology not simply part of people's lives but a way for them to truly view the world without stepping outside their homes. And those who do step outside, head straight for the places they've been watching online."

Rylee knew the business was flourishing and was proud of the work they'd done but had no idea it was this much of a revenue generator. "Well, there is one other thing."

"What might that be?"

She tugged the hem of the short sleeve shirt she wore. "I don't exactly have the wardrobe for Montana."

"No, but if you have a coat that will suffice long enough for you to get from the airport to Brickton, you'll have two days on the company's dime to shop and outfit yourself."

"This is – unbelievable," she admitted. "Seriously. It's –"

"It's us affirming you're part of our family and making it official. So? Will you say yes?"

"How could I not? It's a dream come true. I can't wait to tell my–my brother. Thank you, Ian. Thank you so much. I won't let you down."

"There was never a doubt about that. Now, get cracking. You have two days until the next chapter of your life begins."

Rylee came back to the present with a smile on her face. A new chapter? Yes, it was that. If she did well in Wyoming, she would not just meet her savings goal but surpass it. Which meant she might end up retiring in her forties.

And then what? Her inner voice asked. Rylee tried not to consider the question because she knew what she secretly wished. She wanted to fall in love, to meet someone she could feel about the way her parents felt about one another. They'd married right out of high school, raised two kids, and were crazy about one another for as long as Rylee could remember.

She wanted that. Unfortunately, she'd never fallen in love and was starting to wonder if she ever would. What sort of man was it going to take to knock her off her feet?

The answer to that was a mystery and one she didn't like to contemplate because she truly feared she might be incapable of falling in love. Maybe her brain was wired for the work she did, not for matters of the heart. She had no real problems establishing casual relationships and wasn't in the least shy about letting a man know she was interested. But nothing ever progressed beyond exciting sex at the beginning that lost its appeal when she realized that's all the relationship ever would be.

She was thirty-seven and had never been in love. Maybe the problem wasn't with men but with her. Would she always be alone? Just as she felt herself starting to slide into the fear that inspired, the captain's voice sounded in the cabin, announcing the temperature of Wyoming, and informing the passengers they'd be landing on time.

Shortly after, the announcement was made for everyone to fasten their seat belts. Rylee followed the procedure, eager to land and get a look at the place she was about to call home.

Chapter Two

In her online research, she checked the average temperature in this part of Wyoming in April. The average daytime highs hovered in the fifties and nighttime lows were as far down as twenty-five. Just the thought made her want to tug her jacket closer around her.

The so-called winter coat she thought she had, ended up having two missing buttons and a frayed hem. She didn't have time to go on a coat search before she left, so hoped it would be sunny and in the high fifties when she arrived.

Those thoughts were swept away when she stepped into the terminal. The Jackson Hole, Wyoming, airport must have been designed to stun travelers with the vista beyond the windows. It was breathtaking. There was glass everywhere, presenting a nearly panoramic view of the area. Rylee got so caught up in the scenery as she made her way toward baggage claim, it caught her off guard to see an attractive, middle-aged woman waiting for her at the carousel. The woman held a piece of paper bearing Rylee's name. Rylee walked over to the woman. "Hi, I'm Rylee Monroe."

The woman smiled and extended a hand in greeting. "Well, hello, Rylee Monroe, I'm pleased to meet you. You're much younger than I anticipated but pretty as a picture. I'm Sharon Dillard, Mayor of Brickton, Wyoming."

"Mayor?"

"Is that a surprise?"

"Well, yes and no. Yes, because you're very pretty for a mayor, and I guess I always imagined one as old, male, and bald. But aside from that, as mayor, I imagine you have much more important things to do than greet me."

"Well, honey, I'm also the owner of the condo your company bought for you, so who better to show you around the town and where you'll be calling home?"

"That's very kind of you. I need to claim my luggage, and I'll be ready."

"I can help with that. It should be showing up momentarily."

Rylee followed Mrs. Dillard over to the carousel. "I'm very sorry for your loss, by the way," Mrs. Dillard started another conversation as they waited. "Your colleague, Mr. Corsa, and his partner were lovely people."

"Yes, they were," Rylee had only found out this morning that Brent's partner didn't survive.

"And now here you are, ready to jump in and take over, yes?"

"Yes, ma'am."

"Well, good. You'll be hearing from and seeing me often. I do like to drop in and check to make sure everything's on track, particularly at the change of seasons. You know, we have folks coming here for vacations all year round."

"From what little I saw from the air, and just looking outside now – oh, and the live stream I watched during the flight, I can understand why. It's breathtaking."

"Coming to us from Florida, I imagine you'll feel a bit short of breath once you're out and about. Florida is what, a hundred feet above sea level?"

"Give or take twenty feet, yes."

"Well, here you're six thousand, two hundred feet in elevation. You may feel a bit short of breath or winded at first until you become acclimated."

"Thanks for the heads up. I won't jump out and go for a long run until I acclimate."

"You're a runner?"

"Some. Mostly I bike, and rollerblade, and kayak when I can. Are there places to kayak here?"

"Honey, when you see our lakes and rivers, you'll positively swoon. I'm something of a kayaking fan, myself. You'll have to let me take you out one day."

Rylee smiled and shifted the case with her electronics from one shoulder to the other. "Thank you, I'd love that. Oh there, that's me." She pointed to her luggage.

"Call me Sharon, and let me grab that. You're loaded already." Sharon lifted the piece of luggage off the conveyor belt like it was as light as a handbag. "Is this all?"

"Well, my wardrobe isn't exactly suitable for this climate, so I had most of my stuff shipped. It should be arriving this coming week. Until then, my boss said there were places in town where I could find what I needed. I hope he was right."

"He was indeed. Oh, and your vehicle arrived this morning." Sharon slid the strap of her oversized handbag from her shoulder and dug around in it. "Ha, got it." She pulled out a key fob, and on it were two keys.

"The key to the condo and your office. What do you want to see first?"

"The condo, if that's okay."

"Perfect. Here we go."

On the way out of the airport and during the drive, Sharon told Rylee about the town, the area, the people and answered all the questions Rylee asked. Rylee felt like she was receiving a thorough crash course in everything that was Brickton, Wyoming. Surprisingly, she found herself enjoying the conversation and the drive.

She also found herself liking Sharon Dillard, who was, by all accounts, an open book when it came to her own life. Before they reached Brickton, Rylee knew that Sharon and her husband, Earl, had been married for thirty-five years, had three grown boys who all still lived in Brickton, and one daughter who lived in Iowa with her husband and three daughters.

Sharon had been mayor for a decade, she and Earl owned a hotel and several condos in town, and she loved to fish and hunt, kayak, and camp. She grew up on a ranch, but now two of her sons lived there and ran it. Sharon's father died five years ago, and she moved her mother to a place near town, next door to her and Earl.

It was clear the woman had a big heart, loved her family and town, and was kind to strangers. "What do you think so far?" She interrupted Rylee's thoughts. "Pretty spectacular, isn't it?

Rylee turned her attention back to Sharon. "Honestly, it's like something you'd see in a magazine or a movie, almost too beautiful to be real."

Sharon grinned. "You know, oddly enough, I still get that feeling when I walk outside and look around, and I've been here my entire life."

"Where is your ranch?"

Sharon pointed. "About twelve miles that way. Prettiest land you've ever seen. I'll take you out there sometime if you like. We still have horses if you like to ride."

"I haven't ever ridden a horse, so I don't know."

"Well, we'll teach you. And here we are, Brickton, Wyoming."

"Oh my, it's like riding through the videos I've been watching. What a lovely town."

"Isn't it?" Sharon pointed ahead and to the left. "See right there, that group of buildings that look like a cluster of little houses? That's the condo complex. Each garage creates a barrier between buildings and allows for every unit to have a nice, screened patio and small back yard."

"It's within walking distance of everything," Rylee said excitedly. She hated having to drive everywhere and had often wished she could live somewhere she could ride her bike or walk to a store or restaurant. It looked as if that dream had become a reality.

She pulled out her phone, took a photo, and texted it to her mother. *Would you look at this, mom? It's incredible. I still can't believe I got this promotion. I wish you were here. I bet you'd love it. Will text again later. I love you.*

"Boyfriend?" Sharon asked.

"Mother," Rylee replied as she put her phone away. "I couldn't resist saying how beautiful it is here."

"You'll have to invite her for a visit soon."

"How is the town set for organic produce?" Rylee changed the subject. She liked Sharon, but she didn't talk about her family or personal life to people until she was confident they were trustworthy.

Once they reached the condo, she found herself delighted with the place. It had a window looking out toward the road, affording her a view of the mountains towering in the distance. In the back was a screened patio, and in the common area, a pool, gym, and an outdoor pavilion with chairs for relaxing.

The interior was furnished with comfortable furniture in the living area, a good solid wood desk where she could set up her home office, a gas fireplace, fully outfitted kitchen, right down to pots, pans, and dishware, and a master bath that boasted of a walk-in shower big enough for two people with double water jets.

The bedroom featured a king-size bed and a big window looking out in the same direction as the one in the living area, only giving more of a view of the mountains than the town due to it being upstairs.

There was also a guest room with a queen-size bed and its own bathroom.

"This is beautiful," she said as she put her carry-on and shoulder bag on the bed. "I appreciate you being willing to sell it."

"I made a tidy profit, so I'm not complaining." Sharon smiled and hefted the big suitcase onto the bed. "So, do you want to unpack or grab some lunch and shop? I set aside the rest of the day in case you want a guide and some company."

"I'd love that. Thank you, Sharon. You're so kind to give up your time like this."

"It's what friends do, and I believe that's what we're becoming."

That touched Rylee, and before she considered her actions, she clasped the mayor's hand. "Thank you. I sure hope so."

"No hope to it, it's already happening," Sharon gave Rylee's hand a squeeze before releasing it. "So, the next and one of the most important questions I'll ever ask. Do you eat meat?"

"Is the Pope Catholic?" Rylee quipped and headed downstairs.

Sharon grinned. "Then get ready for some of the best food you've ever had in your life. My brother Jim and his wife, Kate, own and run the best restaurant in town – well, in my opinion, I should add. It's not a fancy place, but you won't find better food anywhere, and the price won't give you indigestion."

"Sounds like my kind of place. Let's go." She opened the front door and held it for Sharon. "Can we walk?"

"Or you could try out your new wheels."

Rylee had completely forgotten about the vehicle. "Oh, I forgot, where is it?"

"See that pretty blue Subaru Outback beside my truck?"

"That's mine?"

"It is. Ready to go try it out?"

"No, I think I'd rather wait until I have a chance to read the manual."

"Ah, one of those, eh?" Sharon chuckled.

"What can I say? I'm a geek," Rylee wasn't offended.

"Then I'll drive. Besides, you might need space for all that stuff you're going to buy."

Rylee laughed. "Well, considering that I work long hours and have one friend, I don't reckon I'm going to need much. My work clothes will be fine with a sweater or jacket, and my boss said those things were being shipped today by the people packing up my house in Orlando. I should have everything in a few days."

"Oh, you'll need new stuff, child. And trust me, you'll make friends here. How could you not with me as your friend?"

"Good point. Okay, let's go stuff our faces then shop 'till we drop. I just need to call No Limits and let them know I'm here and will meet with them on Monday."

"Have at it."

Rylee quickly placed the call, spoke with a woman named Lynda, who was quite friendly, then slid her phone into her handbag. "I'm ready. Let's do this."

"That's my girl. Let's go."

When they stepped outside, Rylee stopped and looked around. She'd never considered herself as anything special, but today she sure felt blessed. She hated that her good fortune came at the cost of someone else's life but was determined to do such a good job that her big fat salary ended up being just a starting place.

And like her parents always told her, everything begins in the mind. If you can see it and you work for it, you can make it happen. That's what she was going to do. Here in, of all places, Wyoming.

Chapter Three

A chorus of greetings rang out the moment Rylee and Sharon entered The Eatery surprised Rylee. It'd been a while since she spent time in a small town. She spent most of her adult life in Orlando, which was, by-and-large, a tourist city. Since she lived just outside the city, the little Mom-and-Pop restaurants in the small towns had been steadily disappearing. There were local restaurants the natives frequented, but no places the tourists didn't find, so this hometown friendliness had become a thing of the past, except in rural areas.

"Well, hey there," an attractive woman with brown hair pulled back into a long-braided ponytail, hurried over and hugged Sharon. "I wasn't expecting to see you today."

"Today's a special day," Sharon ended the embrace and gestured toward Rylee. "This is Rylee Monroe, she's taking over for Mr. Corsa."

"Oh, I am so sorry about Brent," the woman said. "He was a nice man, always so polite and with a pocket full of silly jokes."

Rylee smiled. She'd forgotten that trait of Brent's, and was grateful to be reminded. It said something about this woman that she considered his jokes silly, but obviously endearing. "He was a good person," Rylee replied. "And it's nice to meet you…"

"Kate," The woman filled in the missing information. "Sharon's sister-in-law. My other half is in the kitchen right now.

It's good to meet you and I hope we'll be seeing a lot of you. If there's anything you need help with to get settled, just give a yell."

"Thank you, that's kind. And oh, my goodness, what is that smell, and can I get a vat of it?"

Kate laughed. "That's Jim's pulled chicken, the special of the day, and I'm sure a half dozen steaks on the grill."

"I'm getting weak," Sharon cut in. "Give us a table, and feed us."

"Yes, you look a bit feeble," Kate teased. "Take that table by the window. What do you want to drink?"

"You know I want a diet coke," Sharon replied. "What about you, Rylee?"

"Do you have bottled water?"

Kate and Sharon both laughed, and Rylee realized people were paying attention, which made her feel a bit ill at ease. "I don't get it."

"Nothing says tourist or "not from here" like asking for bottled water," Kate answered.

"Oh, yes, I understand. Still, do you have bottled water?"

"Yeah, we have it. Tourists, you know." Kate rattled off the brands of water, and Rylee made her selection.

As she and Sharon made their way through the restaurant to the table by the window, Rylee couldn't help but notice how many people watched them. She bet they were locals curious about the strange woman with the mayor.

23

Tourists wouldn't care one way or another. She learned that working at the theme parks in Florida during the summers while she was home from college. Locals, however, in a place with as small a population as Brickton, would be understandably curious.

She spent her childhood in small towns, in North Carolina and Georgia, and there she learned how much attention newcomers received from the people who still lived in the old sections of town. In the places she'd seen since then, she realized that people who lived in small congregations tended to be more of a closed society. They were leery of outsiders, and only placed trust in those they'd known all their lives.

That wasn't a criticism as far as she was concerned. She understood the comfort that lifestyle could provide. That sense of belonging and community had its appeal. And she also understood the people who couldn't remain in the small town once they were grown and ready to build their own lives.

Opportunities weren't always plentiful in a small town. People took jobs in the closest cities, and either spent their days grumbling over having to "fight traffic" to and from work, or stopped battling the aggravation and moved closer to the city. They became part of a different social arena, where you develop a network or circle of associates and friends, but you might also not know the names of the people who live four houses down from you.

Rylee wasn't sure what appealed to her. Right now, she felt like she had a big sign on her forehead that flashed "outsider" and she wasn't enjoying it. She caught herself right before she looked at the floor, because she literally heard her mother's voice in her head. *Who doesn't appreciate someone giving them a friendly smile and asking about their day?*

That brought about the shift in attitude she needed to navigate this part of her adventure. One day the locals would see her and say, "oh yeah, that's that girl who works over at the video place, you know, the one that sends out all the live video everywhere?"

But for now, she was a stranger having lunch with the mayor. So, she'd be a friendly stranger. As they passed a table of three women, she smiled and said good morning to at each of them and did that to the next person who looked directly at her. By the time she took her seat, at least three people in the place had returned the smile.

Not a bad start, she thought and looked at Sharon.

"This is such a pretty place. It feels so… welcoming."

Sharon laughed, ignoring the people who glanced her way. "Is that what you call it? I call it being eaten up with curiosity. They're all wondering who you are, and no one has figured out a way to ask, but trust me, before we leave, someone will have texted or called someone and try to figure out who the young woman is with the mayor."

Rylee smiled. "Well, you're lucky I'm female, then. If I were male, they'd think you were having a fling."

Sharon chuckled. "Now wouldn't that set tongues to wagging?"

"Here's your drinks," Kate showed up at the table. Just as she placed the drinks on the table, a voice rang out.

"Where is he? Them people said they have a new boss, who's with the mayor, so where is he?"

"Jim!" Sharon called out as she got to her feet and headed in the man's direction. At the same time, a tall, burly man stepped from behind the bar. "Get him into the office," Sharon ordered.

What in the world was going on? Rylee watched as the man Sharon called Jim approached the upset man with his arms outspread. The gesture communicated both openness and closing a passage. "Ethan, you need to settle down now. Let's go into the office and see if we can square this away."

"I know he's here, and they have footage. I need that footage to—"

"I know, I know," Jim interrupted and guided Ethan down a hallway and out of sight.

Sharon spoke with Kate, who stood watching and then hurried to Rylee. "Come with me."

Rylee didn't question, she merely rose and followed Sharon the way the two men had gone. When Sharon knocked on a door at the end of the hall, a voice sounded with an invitation to enter.

Inside were the man who'd come into the bar, Ethan, and the big man Jim, who Rylee assumed was Sharon's brother. That thought had her looking more closely at him. Sure enough, he and Sharon resembled one another. The eyes, the shape of the lips, there was a resemblance.

Sharon addressed the upset man. "Ethan, the Chief of Police told you already that as soon as we have some answers, we'll let you know. But running all over town and kicking up a ruckus isn't going to help."

"I need answers, Mayor. He was—" Ethan broke down and his tears prompted a gathering of tears in Rylee's eyes.

"He's gone. Donny's gone. He's... He was my only boy."

Those words had the tears spilling out onto her cheeks. Rylee quickly wiped her eyes. "Mr.? I'm sorry, I don't know your last name."

"Caldwell," Ethan replied, and wiped his face on the inside of the arm of his shirt.

"Mr. Caldwell, I'm Rylee Monroe and I'm so sorry for your loss. I don't understand this situation, but heard you say there's footage of something. Is that correct?"

"Yes, those cameras are on all the time, you know. So, one of them had to record what happened."

"What exactly did happen, if I can ask."

"Someone ran down my boy, Donny. Right there in the street. Ran him down like an animal and left him to–to die."

Shock had Rylee frozen in place, and for a few moments there was only the sound of Ethan's snuffles. Sharon spoke up, easing the discomfort. "Rylee, Ethan's son was killed in a hit-and-run. We reckoned the cameras would have footage of it and lead us to the identity of the driver, but No Limits says they don't have any footage for that day, not for any of the cameras."

"No, that's not possible," Rylee said. "We have redundant backups and–"

"You're the new boss?" Ethan interrupted.

The words weren't out of his mouth when the door opened, drawing everyone's attention. Before her mind could do more than register the interruption, and the way everyone stared at the man who filled the door frame, he looked at her.

Rylee wasn't much of a romantic, so when an energy crackled its way over her skin, like static electricity, she marveled at the phenomenon before recognizing the sensation for what it was. Desire.

The man looked away and the moment ended. Rylee quickly turned her attention to Sharon., who addressed the man. "Brick, this is–"

"Is it true?" He stepped into the room. Impossibly, the room felt a little smaller. Rylee made note of that and tried to focus on his question. *Is what true?* His next words ended her confusion.

"Sharon, is it true? Is there footage or not? When is the new man from No Limits going to show up? We pay those people a king's ransom. The least they could do is get a replacement out here to square away this mess."

Sharon cleared her throat before answering. "Brick, let me introduce you to Rylee Monroe, the new Director of No Limits. She's just arrived. Rylee, meet Councilman Ike Brickman, affectionally known as Brick to his friends."

When he turned his gaze on Rylee, she stepped back before realizing she'd moved. What was it about this man? It took a moment to refocus. "Mr. Brickman," she nodded in his direction to demonstrate respect and hopefully help cool his temper, which seemed to be heating up a bit.

"Sir, I'd like to tell you that I have everything under control, but the truth is, I didn't know anything about missing footage or a hit-and-run until about five minutes ago, and I still don't have the entire story.

"But what I do have is enough for me to ask Mayor Dillard's permission to leave, so I can go to No Limits and get started trying to figure out why there is no footage for a specific date. Mayor Dillard, can you text me the date and location? I'll start with the servers and tomorrow will visually inspect the cameras."

"Sounds like a sensible plan," Sharon agreed. "Brick?"

"Fine. But make it quick. Ethan deserves to know who killed his boy."

"I understand and will do my best." She turned to Ethan. "I promise."

"I'll walk out with you," Sharon said and took Rylee's arm.

Neither of them spoke until they were outside, then Rylee leaned in closer to Sharon. "Who was that?"

"Brick? I shouldn't call him that in front of you, that's a name we gave him as kids because he couldn't pass up a dare, was either fearless or dense, and so was always getting into scrapes, getting hurt or in trouble. He was as hard as a brick – physically and mentally. Anyway, he's on the city council and arguably one of the most powerful men in the county, if not the state. His family founded this town, and thus it was named after them in a fashion.

"His family has owned the most successful performance and cow horse breeding ranch in the state for five generations. It didn't start as one of the biggest, but Ike, like his father and grandfather, is an astute businessman. They all made a habit of buying up as much land as they could if it was adjacent to their own.

"He has a daughter and two sons, none of whom are married, much to his chagrin, since he'd love to have grandchildren. He's a fair man, but not a particularly patient one, and just in case you're thinking what many women before you have thought, he has his share of lady friends, but isn't in the market for a wife."

"Neither am I. I was actually curious why he issues orders, and no one objects."

Sharon shrugged. "All too often, he says what the rest of us are thinking, but hesitant to say. Ike isn't hesitant, at all. He's a straight-forward, no bullshit type of man, if you know what I mean."

Rylee nodded, thinking he was also damn hot. But she didn't share that opinion with the mayor. "Well, if you'll point me in the right direction, I'll head for No Limits and dive in. And Sharon, I honestly had no idea there was an issue with the footage. Had I known, I would have insisted on going to the office as soon as I arrived."

"No one's blaming you, Rylee. It's just odd, and maybe it's even a case of your computers being tampered with. Whatever the case, we need to get to the bottom of it."

"Yes, we do, so where am I headed?"

"Don't you want a ride?"

"No, but thanks. It's not cold and I like to walk.

"Suit yourself," Sharon pointed across the street. "Down the block on the left. How are you getting back to the condo?"

" I can walk. It can't be more than a mile. That'll give me a chance to look around and get the feel of the place. Besides, I may want to walk back and forth to work. If–" she paused, then finished around a smile. "I have the breath for it."

As hoped, Sharon grinned. "Smart ass. Fine. Take my number and call if you need me."

"Thanks, Sharon, for everything," Rylee dug her phone out of her purse. "I'll let you know as soon as I have answers. But fair warning, it could take a few days."

"Here, let me put it in." Sharon held out her hand and Rylee handed her the phone.

Sharon quickly programmed in her cell, home, and office phone numbers, along with her email and address, then returned the phone to Rylee.

"Thanks," Rylee slid the phone back into her purse. "I'll be talking to you soon."

"Yes, indeed. Take care."

"You too."

Rylee headed in the direction Sharon indicated. This certainly wasn't the way she imagined her new job starting, and she wanted to talk to her boss, Ian Grant, to find out if he'd been told anything about the missing data.

But that would have to wait until Monday. She checked her iWatch. Three o'clock. That meant she had until Monday to figure out what had gone wrong. She wasn't worried about the contract with the town. They'd salvage that if trouble rose over the missing data. Her goal was to find that data and discover who had killed Ethan Caldwell's son.

It wouldn't bring his son back, but maybe if the guilty party was made to pay, it would bring him justice. That's what she was going to try and make happen.

Chapter Four

Sharon turned and almost collided with Ike Brickman. "Where's she headed?" Ike jerked his head in Rylee's direction.

"To her office. She wants to get started trying to recover the missing data."

"Walking?"

"I offered her a ride. She said she wanted to walk."

"Isn't she a little young? The other guy was older."

"She's old enough. And brilliant. You'd know that if you'd paid attention to the copy of the dossier we received from No Limits' headquarters."

"Still, she seems… green." Ike continued to watch Rylee make her way down the sidewalk.

"Well, she's green to Wyoming, but not to the job. Give her a chance."

"Never said I wasn't going to, Sharon."

"Fine. Then I guess I'll be seeing you at the next council meeting."

"If not before, and the Cattleman's Association has a meeting coming up. I'm guessing you or Earl will be there?"

"To be honest, I've about hit my fill with those things. Too much testosterone. Earl will be there."

"I'll look forward to seeing him."

"Well, I'm headed home, so you have a good weekend."

"If you get any news from that gal—"

"Rylee. Rylee Monroe." She interrupted.

"Right. If you hear from Miss Monroe, you'll let me know?"

"You know I will. Bye, Ike."

She headed for her car. Ike stood on the sidewalk for a moment, considering the events of the last hour. He didn't know how Ethan was holding up as well as he was. Ike's kids might have made him feel like punching his fist through a wall once or twice, but God knew he'd not survive losing one of them. Parents aren't supposed to outlive their children.

And children shouldn't grow up without a mother. That voice in his head sounded an awful lot like his father. Probably because his father and mother drove him half-crazy when his wife left. They figured he needed to find another wife, a woman who'd want to be good to his kids. It took years to convince them to stop the nagging.

Ike wasn't of a mind to get married again. Once was gracious plenty. His ex-wife Glenda had made sure of that. It wasn't enough that she cheated on him. She had to add insult to injury by cheating on him with his oldest friend.

Yep, Glenda sure kicked that friendship in the teeth, along with any favorable opinion he might once have harbored about marriage.

"You have the look of someone chewing on something foul."

Ike looked around to see the Chief of Police, Joe Rogers

Joe Rogers was a big man. As tall as Ike, which put him at six feet, four, but a good fifty pounds heavier. Ike had never known a more honest man than Joe, or one with a bigger heart and sense of justice. That's why he'd campaigned for Joe every time he'd come up for re-election in the last thirty years.

Now Joe was five years away from retirement, and Ike didn't know if they could find a man as honorable to replace him. "Since when do you work weekends, Joe?"

"Since Kate called and said there was some trouble at The Eatery. Something about Ethan attempting to accost the new No Limits fellow."

"Woman."

"Pardon?"

"It's a woman, not a man. Rylee Monroe. She looks like she's eighteen and wet behind the ears."

"Is that a fact? Well, where is this gal?"

"She headed down to her office."

"The mayor leave already?"

"You just missed her."

"Well, I imagine I'll be talking to her soon enough. Maybe you can help clear up some things for me."

"Like what?"

"Jim said the gal—Miss Monroe, didn't appear to know the footage from the camera had gone missing."

"No, I don't believe she did."

"That's odd. We called the company headquarters and spoke with—dang if I can remember his name. I have it written down. Anyway, we talked with someone who assured us that if they couldn't locate the data remotely, the new person they were sending would be able to retrieve it. I took that to mean the person coming here knew about the problem."

"Apparently not."

"Strange," Joe glanced down the street, then at Ike. "Between you and me, I'm starting to wonder if that data went missing by accident."

"How else could it have disappeared? No one I know has the expertise to break into that place and just take it. Hell, how would someone even know how or where to look?"

"I don't know, Ike, but something is starting to scratch at my brain about this. I'm going to take a closer look at Ethan's son to make sure he wasn't mixed up in something we weren't aware, and if he associated with anyone who might have the skills for something like that."

"Hell, I wouldn't even know what skills it would take. Would you?"

"Not a clue, but I've got people smart enough to help me figure out what that would be."

"Then you better get after it, Joe, because Ethan's barely holding it together."

"Don't I know it. Well, I'm going to grab a sandwich, then head down to speak with Miss Monroe. Want to join?"

"Might as well. I haven't had lunch."

"Then it's on you, my friend."

Ike smiled and patted Joe's shoulder. He might not have a wife waiting on him at home, but he had family and good friends, and that had to be enough.

Now, he just had to get the vision out of his mind, of Rylee Monroe locking eyes with him when he strode into Jim's office. Ike hadn't felt anything like that in years, that punch of attraction that nailed you in the gut and spread all the way through you.

"Say, if the new No Limits lady is a looker, maybe you should introduce her to Tom," Joe said. "To hear your dad tell it, Tom forgets to come home some nights he's so caught up in cowboying. Asa thought Tom was learning to be a rancher."

"Yeah, well, so did I, and he is, just not as fast as Pop and I would like. It seems he likes the life of a cowboy over that of a rancher, and to be honest, Joe, I don't blame him. I miss being a cowboy."

"Don't we all?" Joe asked and laughed. "Yep, those were the days."

"Indeed, they were," Ike agreed, and wondered for the first time if he was letting life pass him by. Was he so focused on the family legacy and the business of ranching that he'd cut himself off from the very thing he loved so much about it? Namely, feeling that attachment to the land and the living things it nourished. That's how cowboying felt to him. It was what he missed.

But then, at his age, there were a lot of things he missed., and some of those things he'd just have to learn to be happy without.

*****

It wasn't hard to find the No Limits office. They had a street-front location, ground floor office. Rylee noticed that the large front window and the door sported decorative metal work over the glass, she assumed as a security feature.

When she opened the door, she was confronted by four people: a woman who sat at a reception desk, three men and another woman who stood in front of the desk. It wasn't hard to figure out that she'd interrupted a conversation.

"Can I help you?" The standing woman turned.

"Hi," Rylee cut straight to the point. "I'm Rylee Monroe, Brent's replacement."

The woman smiled and offered her hand. "Sheila Smith. Hi, Rylee."

"Wow, I expected you to be older." Rylee shook her hand. "It's nice to put a face to the name."

A man who looked to be in his forties, with brown hair cut short, a trimmed beard, dressed in business casual clothing, walked over to her, extending his hand. "Jack Edwards, Ms. Monroe. Software developer."

"And overall security whiz, I hear. It's an honor to meet you, Jack. I've heard good things about you. I hate that our meeting had to arise from a tragedy."

"Same here," he paused and looked at the others. "Let me introduce you. This is Kyle Haley. He's our hardware guru."

"As I hear it, he's a hardware genius," Rylee drew on all the information she'd been given about the team here in Brickton.

"I'll take that compliment," Kyle responded, and hurried to shake her hand. "I've heard about you, as well."

"Nothing horrible, I hope," she noticed his friendly demeanor, and quick smile.

"Just that you're Ian's protégé, and he's fast-tracking you so that someone else doesn't snatch you away from him."

"Wow, I wish I'd known that. I would have asked for more money."

Everyone laughed, and the third man introduced himself. "I'm Howie Evans. I'm the in-the- trenches guy." He looked like a man who spent time outdoors, with more color in his skin and a bit more casual appearance.

"You handle camera set up and maintenance, correct?"

"Yes, ma'am."

"Please, I don't believe in formality. We're a team. And I will admit I'm psyched to be selected to work with the No Limits dream team. I just wish my time here didn't have to begin this way."

She glanced at the woman seated at the desk. "Hi."

"Oh hi, I'm Lynda. Secretary slash receptionist."

"It's nice to meet you, Lynda." She paused for a moment, then jumped right in. "Home office didn't tell me about the hit-and-run, or missing data, so you can imagine my surprise when the father of the fatality tried to accost me at The Eatery.

"I still don't have the entire story, so if you have no objections, I'd suggest we call in some food and you can all bring me up to speed while we eat. Is there a place in town with delivery?"

"The Eatery has delivery," Sheila offered. "I have their takeout menu."

"Then let's get an order made up. For myself, I'd love a club sandwich, fries, and an iced tea the size of Rhode Island. Oh, wait, do they make iced tea in Wyoming?"

"Not sweet tea," Howie answered.

"Ugh, then scratch the tea. I'll take two bottles of water."

"The water is actually good here," Kyle said. "I was hesitant when I arrived, but finally broke down and tried it and stopped buying the bottles."

"Okay, I'll trust you. An extra-large ice water. Lynda, do you have a company card for office expenses?"

"I sure do."

"Then put the food on that."

"Are you sure? Brent–"

"I'm sure. If you need additional authorization, text Mr. Grant."

"No, it will be fine." Lynda wrote down everyone's order and called it in. Once she hung up the phone, Rylee looked around. "Is this the most comfortable place for us to talk and eat?"

"We have a lounge," Howie replied and smiled. "Comes in handy when you're pulling an all-nighter because an ice storm took out four cameras."

"Don't give away all the good stuff too soon, Howie," she teased. "And how about showing me around?"

Rylee was impressed with the offices. Her team gave her the tour before they all settled in the lounge. Talk about impressive. A massive room, it boasted of a fully equipped kitchen and bathroom, with an enormous walk-in shower and lockers. A long bar separated the kitchen from the seating area which was furnished with three big deep cushioned sofas, two wing chairs and a dining room table that would seat a dozen.

"Now this is a lounge," Rylee said appreciatively, and sank onto one of the wing chairs. "Okay, gang, while we wait, I need you to fill me in."

"Where do you want us to start?" Jack asked.

"The day before the event."

"What about it?" Jack asked.

"Just tell me about it. Was there anything different about that day? Anyone out of the ordinary paying a visit, asking for a meeting? Was there anything abnormal about that day?"

Everyone was silent, glancing around at one another. It was clear from the way they looked at each other, there was no fear. They simply couldn't come up with anything to say. That was fine. Rylee just wanted to get a feel for how they reacted and interacted.

"Nothing comes to mind," Jack finally answered.

"Okay, so what about the system? Any glitches, hiccups? Are the backups for that date intact and accessible?"

"No issues with the software," Jack replied immediately.

"And no problems with the hardware," Kyle added. "We run daily diagnostics, as you know. Same procedure as your office in Orlando follows. A diagnostic report is automatically generated and uploaded to home office every twelve hours."

Rylee nodded and looked at Howie. "No issues with the cameras?"

"Nothing."

"Okay, then. So, the day before was business as usual."

Everyone agreed that was a correct assessment. Rylee pulled her phone from her purse and opened a new note, starting a list of things she needed to check into. First on the list was to read the diagnostic reports to ensure nothing was missed.

"So, what about Brent and all of you? Were you all at work the day before and the day of the event? Did anyone get into an argument, a heated discussion? Did anyone talk about problems at home or something that'd happened in town?"

"Where are you going with this?" Sheila asked.

"I'm not sure yet," Rylee admitted. "But here's the deal folks. A young man was run down in the street. His life ended, and his parents' lives were destroyed. The only chance there is of finding out who did that to him could be in the video footage. If it's missing, there must be a reason, and we need to discover what happened. Let's help the Caldwell family get justice."

There was no argument to her statement, and for that, Rylee was grateful. They didn't realize, but her motives were twofold— to help the Caldwell family and to protect No Limits and its employees.

Very wily, Ian. Rylee realized her appointment to this position wasn't made simply for her skills in data mining, design, or cyber security development. She was sent here because Ian knew she'd check every line of code, analyze every report, and run diagnostics on every piece of equipment to find out what had happened to the data.

He also knew that if anyone could identify a hack, it was her. And she wouldn't stop until she found the answer. That was Rylee's Achilles' Heel. She couldn't let a mystery go unsolved, and she'd turn over every stone in the Rockies until she found the solution.

Rylee hoped she'd live up to her reputation, but wondered if Ian's hopes weren't a bit misplaced. She could ferret out a problem with the programming or even the hardware, but knowing what she did about the system, she didn't believe it was a mere glitch. The system was too protected, and a glitch would never have caused it to behave in such a fashion.

There was only one way that data could have gone missing. Someone had to have deleted it. Which meant she wasn't looking for a what, but a who. And as someone who'd been in town all of four hours, that was a very big challenge.

CIANA STONE

Chapter Five

Ike rose as the pickup pulled up in front of the house. "If you're here for supper, I ate about an hour ago."

The man who climbed out of the truck laughed. "Son, why would I ever want to pass up your mama's cooking for what you pass off as supper?"

"I think Bear might take offense at that, Pop. What brings you here?

"Trouble."

That one word was enough to cause Ike to lose his taste for the mug of coffee in his hand. "What kind?"

"The sort that has a grave-digger working more than normal." The pea gravel in the path leading to the house crunched under Asa Brickman's boot soles.

"I don't like the sound of that."

"Didn't reckon you would. Let's go inside."

"Sure." Ike let his father lead the way. This was once Asa's home. It was where Ike, his brother David, and their sister Melody grew up. David was the oldest and supposed to inherit the honor of raising his family in this house, but he died before he married. Melody married the son of a rich man who bought land in Wyoming for a vacation home, moved to New York, and never returned.

Which left the honor to Ike. He'd married and tried raising his kids here, but his wife high-tailed it back to California when their youngest, Matthew, was only two. Ike was ashamed to admit it, but even to this day, he remembered being upset because he wasn't equipped to take care of the kids and be ranch foreman, a position he'd earned and put his heart and soul into. Losing Glenda was a relief. All they ever did was squabble and bicker, and he'd grown bone weary of that.

One tradition the Brickman family followed was to ensure every member earned their rights and privileges. If Ike wanted to one day run Brickman Ranch, he had to earn it. He didn't mind that a bit, but he couldn't do his job well and tend to the kids.

His mother came to the rescue behind his back. She told Asa that she missed having children underfoot, and with that Jezebel gone back to where she belonged, Ike needed some help. Therefore, she wanted to move back to the main house to watch after the kids until Ike found himself another wife.

Ike smiled as he remembered. His kids didn't grow up with a mother, but they grew up surrounded by people who loved them. When Matt graduated from high school, Asa announced it was time he and Georgia moved back home to the river house. And it was way past time Ike thought about finding himself someone to spend time with. A man wasn't supposed to spend his life alone.

At present, Asa had the expression of a man ready to go to war, which told Ike there'd been a threat against someone Asa cared about. "What's going on, Pop?" he asked as soon as Asa sat down in one of the chairs closest to the fireplace.

"Nothing good." Asa propped his right ankle on his left knee, took off his hat, and balanced it on his upright knee. "I hear you met the new No Limits person?"

"Woman. Rylee Morgan."

"Does she know what she's doing, or do we need to call and tell that company to send a man out here to get things squared away?"

Ike opened his mouth, then closed it. He'd almost said he'd had the same thought, but that wasn't entirely true. He had no idea if Rylee Monroe was good at her job but knew that the man at the helm of No Limits was a smart and savvy businessman. He'd built his company from the ground up, and now it was a force to reckon with in security, physical, and cyber, and employed the brightest and most talented people in the industry.

"I figure if they sent her, they consider her to be good."

"She better be. Earl Dillard dropped by, and he said Sharon told him that Monroe gal didn't even know their computers had screwed up and lost the video of what happened to Ethan's boy."

Ike wouldn't lie but didn't want to add any fuel to the fire, so he downplayed it. "I don't think they had much time, and I'd guess the folks who are still here from No Limits will fill her in."

"I guess. But she better use her spurs and get moving fast because folks are getting riled up about it. Earl also said that Monroe gal is a looker and said you met her."

"I did."

"So, is she?"

"Is she what?"

"Are you going deaf? Is she good-looking?"

"Yeah, she looks fine for a young woman."

"How young?"

"Young enough to be your granddaughter." It wasn't until the words were out of his mouth that Ike realized he could have just as easily said *young enough to be my daughter*. What did that signify?

There wasn't time to ponder it because Asa had bitten into the topic like a dog going at a bone. "You know that for a fact?"

"I don't know anything for a fact, Pop, only that she appeared young to me. I guess I was paying more attention to what was going on than how she looked."

The harumph that came out of Asa told Ike that his father wasn't satisfied with the answer but wouldn't push it, which suited Ike. He hadn't yet decided what he thought about Rylee Monroe. Not about her looks. She looked fine. Better than fine.

No, he wasn't going to focus on her looks or the punch her gaze delivered. His focus was on what she said and whether he could believe her. That question would be answered in time, but he thought perhaps he should give her the benefit of the doubt until then. Ike wasn't a scholar, but he was a decent judge of character, and she didn't appear at all disingenuous.

Rather than address that topic, Ike changed the subject. "Matt mentioned you and he were headed over to the park before daylight with the drones to help search for two missing hikers."

WHERE THE MOUNTAINS KISS THE SKY

"Yeah, they wandered off today, and the folks they were with got spooked, so we'll put the birds in the air and see if we can spot them."

"If anyone can find them, it's you and Matt. He's turned into quite the pilot. Drone and manned."

"Indeed, he has." Asa pushed up to a standing position. "And I reckon I'll head on back. Your mama has a fresh apple pie coming out of the oven. Want to join us for a slice?"

"I do, but I won't. I've got a full plate tomorrow and figured I'd turn in early."

"Then I'll leave you to it."

"Let me know if you find those hikers." Ike rose and accompanied his father outside. "And save me a piece of pie."

"If you're lucky, good night, son."

"G'Night Pop. Love to mom."

Ike watched his father leave and stood there a few minutes, gazing up at the sky. He wondered if Rylee Monroe had ever seen this much sky or this many stars. He'd been to Florida, and the one thing he remembered was that there was way too much light, and you couldn't see the stars at night.

Which made it an ill fit for him. Just like that woman.

Ike had a full plate right here on the ranch. The last thing he needed was a complication, and in his experience, that's what women were best at.

*****

It was well past midnight when Rylee's team finished telling her all they could remember about the day of the Caldwell boy's hit-and-run, and the days that followed. There were aspects of the tale that bothered her, but she didn't mention it. Instead, she thanked them for giving up their night and sent them home.

Once they were gone, she went into her office, the office that had belonged to Brent. On a whim, she sat at the desk and started emptying the drawers, one at a time, onto the surface of the desk.

As she sifted through the contents, snippets of conversation floated through her mind. "Brent gave us the afternoon off, and he said he'd take the on-call laptop home with him."

She wondered if that was unusual and wished she'd asked, but today she'd only wanted the people to get comfortable confiding in her. When she spotted a legal pad, she pulled it out of the drawer, grabbed a pen from the small pencil holder on the desk, and started a list. She wrote a reminder to ask whether Brent had ever done that before.

Sheila had commented about the day after the hit-and-run, Rylee made a note of on her page. "I didn't know about the hit-and-run when I got to work. We found out about an hour later when the Chief of Police asked if anyone was working last night and if he could speak with Brent.

"I told him I'd let him know the moment Brent came in. It was strange that he wasn't already here. Brent was always on time – most of the time he was here before any of us."

"That struck me as odd too," Jack added. "Brent was never late."

"Oh, and he looked like he'd been punched," Howie added. "The right side of his face was bruised on his cheekbone.

"You're right, I forgot about that," Sheila exclaimed and looked around at everyone. "I remember us saying something about it at lunch."

"He never did say anything about why he was late," Kyle said. "And even stranger, the next day, I came in at four in the morning to install some new boards that arrived the previous day. All the backups have finished by four, so it's the perfect time for hardware upgrades before the day gets underway.

"What was odd, though, was Brent was already here. When I asked, he said he'd been running diagnostics on the system, and there seemed to be an issue with the weekly backup. He was running a deeper diagnostic, and it would run for at least another hour, so he was going to grab some breakfast."

Kyle looked around at everyone, and so did Rylee. She didn't understand the sudden somber expressions until Kyle spoke again. "That was the day he ran off the road and was killed."

Rylee didn't know what to make of that but made a note on her legal pad. She tore the page off, folded it, and stuck it in her purse that lay on the desk. As she returned the pad to the desk, she noticed something else in the drawer, packaging for a memory card.

She frowned and lay the package on the desk, then scoured the drawer, looking for the card that came in the package. It was not in the drawer. Rylee glanced at the package again. Why would Brent have an empty memory card package in his desk drawer?

Where was the card?

And why was he running diagnostics before four in the morning? She didn't remember seeing anything in the reports about unscheduled diagnostics.

Rylee leaned back and stared across the room. Nothing made sense. What was she missing?

She rubbed her forehead with one hand. Maybe she needed to call it a day. She checked the time and got to her feet, grabbing her purse. She'd go to the condo, grab a few hours' sleep, and then come back and run some diagnostics of her own.

When she stepped outside, the cold air hit her with a near physical impact. Hugging her jacket close around her, she looked up and forgot all about the cold. "Wow." She didn't realize she'd spoken aloud until she heard her own voice. But wow, it was fitting. The sky was endless, filled with stars. It was like an image from a photograph, almost too beautiful to be real.

The dichotomy wasn't lost on her. Five minutes ago, her mind was tangled in a mystery that made her feel very ill at ease. Now all she could do was stare, taken by the sky, and suddenly sensing a connection, and hoping she'd last long enough here to explore her relationship to this place.

Her father taught her that every place has power all its own and lessons to teach. Rylee wondered what lessons Wyoming had in store for her.

Chapter Six

Try as she might, Rylee couldn't sleep. At first, she blamed it on being in a new place. Next, she blamed the bed. Finally, she admitted it had nothing to do with where she was or the brand of mattress. The situation with the missing footage and what her team told her about the day of the hit-and-run had her brain in a spin. There were too many unanswered questions, and she'd get no peace until she found the answers.

She considered getting up, dressing, and heading back to the office, but it wasn't even two in the morning. If she didn't get some sleep, she would be at a disadvantage when it came time to dig into the code and determine if any changes were implemented that could account for the missing data.

A memory surfaced. She'd just started college and was having minor panic attacks. Rylee had never been a popular girl in school, nor did she have many friends. She was told her propensity to get lost in an algorithm made her seem unapproachable.

That didn't make much sense to her, but social interaction had always been something of a challenge. And most people didn't even understand what an algorithm was. Her dad said her brain was wired kind of like a computer. Computers depend on complex algorithms or sequences of instructions, where the goal is to solve a specific problem, perform a particular action or computation. In a way, the algorithm is a clear specification for processing data or doing calculations, along with other tasks.

He said that's the way her mind worked, and she couldn't change that, nor should she want to. She would meet people who could appreciate her for who she was and not care if she got lost in processing data or making sure an algorithm was sound.

Her mother advised her to try and find ways to fit in. Rylee did that when she went to college, but the more she tried, the more anxious she felt. Her mother tried to help by teaching her relaxation techniques. It took her an entire semester of practice, but finally, it paid off, and she got the panic attacks under control.

Now she used the technique her mother taught her, lay flat on her back, closed her eyes, and started taking slow breaths, in for a count of three and out for a count of twelve. Little by little, she increased the length of her exhales until she took three breaths a minute. Rylee felt relaxation seeping in, making her muscles loosen. The swarm of questions became words on bright balloons, rising into an endless sky.

Rylee jerked awake, not sure how long she'd been asleep until she glanced at the clock on the nightstand. It was almost six. Four hours wasn't enough sleep to have her feeling entirely rested, but she could function well enough.

Throwing back the covers, she rose and headed for the bathroom. Half an hour later, she was showered, dressed, and headed into the kitchen. "Oh great," she grumbled when she started searching the cabinets. Buying supplies was on the list of things she never got around to yesterday, thanks to the revelation about the hit-and-run.

Hopefully, there would be coffee at the office. Holding that in mind, she headed out. "Holy crap." Her lightweight jacket wasn't nearly enough to keep her from shivering in the cold. She'd intended to walk to the office, but the temperature changed her mind, so she opted to drive the new SUV.

The obsessive side of her nature balked at driving it before she'd read the manual cover-to-cover, but not even her OCD would force her to walk in the cold. At least not until she had a decent coat to wear.

To her relief, the car was toasty warm before she reached the stoplight in the center of town. As she waited for the light to turn green, she looked around and realized The Eatery was open. There were cars parked in the lot, and through the windows, she could see people.

That meant freshly brewed coffee. Rylee made the turn and parked in the lot beside the restaurant. After the warmth of the vehicle, the outdoor temperature seemed even colder. She hurried into the restaurant and was surprised to be greeted by name the moment she walked in.

"Good morning, Rylee," Kate said with a smile. "How was your first night?"

"A challenge," Rylee responded honestly but didn't elaborate.

Kate laughed. "New places always are. Want to sit at the bar or a table?"

"I hate to take up a table just for me, so the bar."

"Well, pick a stool. Coffee?"

"Yes, a vat please."

"Coming up."

Rylee peeled off her jacket, draped it on the back of the stool, pulled her phone from her purse, and looped the messenger bag on the back of the chair. Kate put a big mug of coffee in front of her. "Cream and sugar?"

"Cream please."

"Regular or French vanilla."

"Oh, I think I love you. French vanilla, please."

"You got it." Five seconds later, Kate placed a little pitcher of creamer in front of Rylee. Once her coffee was suitably doctored, Rylee sipped it and sighed. "Heaven in a cup."

"Want some breakfast? Jim makes the fluffiest waffles in two states."

"Ooh, you talked me into it. Thanks."

When Kate moved away, Rylee picked up her phone and started texting her parents. She told them she survived her first night in Wyoming, was determined to find a coat before sunset, and had met all the people she'd be working with, and they were all pleasant. She hit send, lay the phone aside, and turned her attention back to her coffee.

"This seat taken?" A male voice had her glancing to her left. The man who stood beside her could have been a model for a "come to Wyoming" ad. From his cowboy hat to his boots, he looked every inch the hero from a romance novel. Handsome, well-built, and eyes that were darn near electric blue.

"No, it's free."

"Do you mind?"

Wow, good looks, and manners. Now that was a nice combination. "Not at all."

He sat and gave her a smile. "Tourist?"

"Me?" She understood why he'd ask. She wasn't dressed like a local. "No, I just moved here for work and didn't have time to shop for winter clothes before the move."

"What kind of work?"

"The director's position of No Limits."

"My condolences on the death of your business associate."

Rylee wasn't sure it was wise to open a discussion, but she'd been told little about what happened to Brent. "We weren't given much information. Was the accident a collision? Was anyone else hurt?"

"Here you go," Kate set a mug of coffee in front of Matt. "You ready to order?"

"Gimme a minute?"

"Okay, holler when you're ready."

"Thanks, Kate." He sampled the coffee, sighed in what Rylee perceived as pleasure, and then turned his attention back to her. "The way I hear it, there was a problem with his car, and he went off the road. The stretch of road he was on isn't what you'd call treacherous, but there are places where you'd want to be mindful of your speed. Especially if it's raining."

"Was it raining that day?"

"To be honest, I don't know."

"Oh, that's okay, I just wish I knew what happened. But I don't guess I'll figure that out. Maybe I can at least help uncover what happened to the Caldwell boy."

"I hope so. Oh, pardon my manners. I'm Matt Brickman."

"Rylee Monroe," she offered her hand.

"It's a pleasure, Ms. Monroe? Or is that Mrs.?"

"It's Ms. And I'm pleased to meet you. I think I may have met someone in your family yesterday. Ike Brickman?"

"Yep, that's my dad."

Rylee nodded, realizing she did see a family resemblance. Both were tall, well-built, blue-eyed, and handsome. That wasn't an observation she'd share aloud, but she would ponder the similarities and differences at some point in time. Right now, she replied with a conversationally safe remark. "So, the Mayor said your family owns a ranch. Are you a cowboy or…?"

"I reckon I am – at least part-time, but mostly, I fly."

"Fly? As in planes?"

"Some. Mostly helicopters and drones."

"Really?" Rylee was fascinated with drone piloting and was considering trying to get her license. "What type of drone piloting? "

"Fire and rescue, mapping, and real estate for the most part. Last year we shot a car commercial near Teton. Are you interested in piloting?"

"I am."

"Well, if you want to learn, let me know, and I'll take you out and show you the basics."

"Seriously?"

"Yeah, sure."

"That's very kind. Thanks. I just may take you up on that."

"Then put my number in that phone and give me a call when you're ready."

"Oh, yes, thanks," she grabbed her phone, entered the number he recited, and then sent him a text.

He pulled his phone from his pocket and smiled. "Now you have my number," she said. "If you ever want to learn about cyber security or how to hack."

"Hack? As in computers?"

"Yes."

"You're a hacker?"

"Not at present."

"Implying you have been at some time in your life?"

She lifted her coffee mug to her face. "No, comment."

Matt just smiled. "That's cool, but I am curious, how does someone learn to do that?"

"Cyber security?"

"No, be a hacker."

She sipped from her mug. "Be the best at cyber security."

"Want to clarify?"

Rylee angled slightly toward him. "If you understand how the security works, you can figure out a way around it. So, if you become the best at designing the systems, you will be adept at breaking into them."

Matt grinned. "You almost make it sound intriguing. But let's say a person wanted to learn how to do that. Where do you start?

"Like anything else. Go to school. Study. Read. Join the online forums and groups and ask a million questions. Be patient and worm your way into a higher-level group, one with experienced hackers, and learn from them, find out what others have done, and figure out how to either break their code or make it stronger."

"Did you do that?"

She smiled. "I've been learning since I was nine. My father was a systems analyst who designed accounting systems for big corporations. He started teaching me to code, and I was mesmerized with the logic, with writing commands that caused a machine to perform a specific task. It seemed like a type of magic."

"You sure make it sound like it."

She looked away, a bit uncomfortable at having revealed something so personal about herself to a stranger. He seemed to perceive her discomfort and asked, "Does your company do that? Design security that's hard to break into?"

"Yes." She smiled in relief, and the smile he offered in return seemed to offer something she hadn't had in a long time. Friendship.

"And you also break systems. For companies."

"Not exactly. We will attack their security if hired to do so, and we'll be relentless. There've been times when the battle was fierce enough that the corporation who hired us lost their entire system."

"That had to have pissed them off. Who wants to pay someone to destroy your stuff?"

"Oh, we didn't destroy the real system. Only a copy. We cloned their entire setup – machines, programming, right down to the type of cables used. And we burned it down, so to speak."

"And you loved it."

She looked away and was surprised when he gave her arm a nudge. "Come on, admit it. You loved it."

"Yes, I did," she confessed.

"And that's how you'd choose to spend your time, given a choice?"

Rylee considered the question. "No. Not all the time. No one can ride that type of high for long. As exciting and challenging as it is, it's not healthy to sit there for hours on end, never breaking focus. When you lose focus – you lose that nanosecond, and that's all it takes to close the door on you, and you have to start over."

After a sip of coffee, she continued. "I'd gladly take a project like that, but only maybe once a year. The rest of the time, I'm content to be a sort of white hacker, help businesses detect gaps in network security, and help protect the company from cybercrimes."

"And how do you accomplish that?"

"We go through their security to detect vulnerabilities, solve them, and create defenses before cybercriminals can find them."

"Impressive, and you personally do that?"

"Yes."

"Then you should be able to determine if your systems were hacked and the data was stolen, right?"

The question took her off guard. Why would he ask that? "Yes," she tried to set aside the notion that he'd deliberately led her to this question. "I should."

Her curiosity overcame everything else. "But why would you think there was a breach in our security? Was the boy that was killed into something illegal? What would make someone want to take the footage if, in fact, it was taken?"

"Beats the heck out of me. Nothing much makes sense about this thing."

"That makes two of us," she looked away as she commented. Had he just tried to trip her up or help her? No one had said anything about a need to hack No Limits. What would be the purpose? They were as much a victim as the hit-and-run.

Rylee turned her gaze to Matt again, and for a moment, they just stared at one another. "Let me ask you something else," Matt said as a smile started to rise on his face. "Could you hack the transmission from a drone?"

"In a snap, but why the question?"

"Just wondering. Those birds are expensive, and I'd hate to think someone could bring it down without even touching the controls."

"It'd be a complicated hack, and unless you're filming something classified or illegal, I doubt it would be worth the cost of hiring someone."

"Good to know, but let me ask one more question. Is there a way to protect it from being hacked?"

"Absolutely."

"Do you think you could make a recommendation on someone who can do that?"

Rylee considered the question for a few moments. Was this a hand of friendship being extended or a subterfuge? She didn't know. Yet. In time, she would. But for now, it didn't hurt a thing to go, as her mother would say, with the flow.

"Yes, me." She finally answered.

"I wasn't asking for a favor, I –"

"I know, I didn't take it that way, but I'd be interested in a trade."

"What kind?"

"You teach me to pilot, and I'll make sure your birds are protected."

"Girl, you've got a deal." He stuck out his hand.

Rylee smiled and clasped it. "But before I can get started, I have to solve a mystery at work."

"The missing data?"

"Yes, by the way, did your father say something about that?" She wondered how many people in town were talking about it.

"No, but it's not exactly a secret. The police were at your office the next day asking for video."

"Naturally, I would expect that."

"So, can you use your Ninja hacking skills and find it?"

Rylee laughed. "I don't know. Until this morning, I never considered using my Ninja hacking skills against the people who sign my paycheck."

"Then call and ask their permission. If they don't have anything to hide, they'll say yes. Don't you want to try?"

Rylee liked his logic but didn't say it. Instead, she answered as honestly as she could without acknowledging the accusation. "Yes, but there are many factors to be taken into account."

"Like what?"

"A lot of things, but most notably whether the cameras were on and recording during that time, or if the data was deleted."

"How will you figure it out?"

"Dive into the system and see what I find."

"Sounds..." he smiled. "Way above my head. Man, that looks good."

Rylee glanced in the direction of his gaze as Kate placed a plate in front of her bearing the biggest waffle she'd ever seen. It covered the entire plate, and a massive glob of butter in the center spread out in golden streams.

"That's enormous. I'll never eat all this." She looked at Matt. "Want to split it with me?"

"Are you kidding? I never turn down food."

"Can I get another plate, Kate?"

"Sure thing."

Two minutes later, Rylee and Matt were wolfing down the most delicious waffle she'd ever tasted, smothered in fresh butter and hot syrup. "This is too good," she commented between bites. "Now I'll be craving it, and before summer comes, I'll be a dough girl."

Matt grinned. "Not if you only eat it once a week and split it with a friend."

"You know, I have a feeling we're going to be. Friends, that is."

"Yep, we sure are."

Rylee smiled and speared another chunk of waffle. Last night, all she could do was fret about the missing data and the hit-and-run. Now, even though she'd put all her professional energy and expertise into trying to solve the mystery, here she was, having breakfast with a handsome pilot-slash-cowboy.

Today wasn't starting off so bad, after all.

CIANA STONE

Chapter Seven

Rylee and Jack sat across from one another at the conference room table. That's where they'd spent most of their time the last three weeks. Now at almost three o'clock on Thursday, the answer they'd sought finally revealed itself.

She and Jack glanced at each other simultaneously. "It makes no sense," Jack commented.

"That data was taken from the system, or that we weren't even aware of it?"

"That it happened. What possible benefit could it be to erase twenty-four hours of video footage?"

Rylee's mind flashed back to the empty storage card contained in Brent's desk. "Hey, are you listening?" Jack's voice snapped her back to the present.

"Yes. And if I had to speculate, I'd guess whoever did this didn't care about the entire day, but one specific block of time."

"Why?"

"Because the missing footage could possibly have revealed the license plate, or maybe even the driver of the vehicle that stuck the Caldwell boy."

"Someone wants to cover their ass." Jack pushed back from the computer. "But how? Seriously, Rylee, how could someone have done this? You know this system as well as I. Hell, you were the lead designer if I remember correctly. So, tell me, do you believe your code is that easy to break?"

"No, I don't." She didn't say it with conceit, simply as a fact. There were a lot of things she couldn't do or was not good at, but in this, she was more than capable, and she knew there was no weakness in the system's defense.

"The system is sound. You and I know that. We've been through everything, and the truth is, this wasn't a hack, and no one broke the security."

"Then what was it?"

"Whoever deleted the footage had a key."

Jack's eyebrows rose. "No one here would do that. I mean, aside from you and me, who has the skill?"

"Brent did."

"Brent's dead."

"Yes, I know. And don't you find his death just a bit suspicious?"

"No, it was a car accident." Jack stood and stretched before continuing. "Look, I know everyone wants to find out who was responsible for the hit-and-run, but it's reaching to even consider Brent was somehow involved."

Rylee disagreed but wasn't going to argue. She needed a moment or two to consider what she'd learned and decide what her next step would be.

"I suppose I'm just tired," she said, closed and picked up her laptop. "You must be as well. We've been at it for over twelve hours a day for the last three weeks. Take the rest of the day off, and tomorrow as well, if you want, Make it a long weekend. You've earned some downtime."

"I won't pass that up."

"You sound like a man who already had an idea of how he wants to spend his weekend."

"I do. I have a sweet fifth wheel and love to camp every chance I get. In my downtime, I like doing nature and wildlife photography, and this is one of the best places in the country for that."

"Then get at it," she said, then added. "And when you're back, let's have lunch or a beer, and you can maybe show me some of your photos."

"Really?"

"Yes, I'd like to see this place through your eyes."

"That'd be great, and thanks for the extra time off."

"You've more than earned it. Thanks, Jack. Have a great weekend."

"You too."

Rylee watched him hurry out of the room, then headed to her office. She put the laptop in the messenger bag she'd carried since her parents gave it to her. Maybe it would be wise to give herself the rest of the day off, or at least get a change of scenery. She needed a clear head to consider what she and Jack discovered and decide how to handle it.

And the best way she knew to get that clarity was to get outside and get some fresh air. Rylee tugged on the coat Mayor Sharon had brought her, looped the strap of her messenger bag across her body, and left the office. She stopped at her secretary's desk. "Lynn, I'm going to call it a day. I'll have my cell if there's an emergency. And Jack is off until Monday, so don't direct any calls to him until then."

"Okey dokey," Lynn, a bubbly blonde with a passion for romance novels about firemen, smiled. "Have a good evening."

"You too," Rylee returned the smile and stepped outside. Today was warm enough that she felt a little too toasty in the coat, so when she unlocked her car, she removed the coat and tossed it into the back seat, took her phone from her messenger bag, then locked the bag in the car.

Rylee didn't have a destination in mind, she just wanted to be outside. So, she headed down the sidewalk in the direction of the Town Hall. There was a charming park with trails, and today was perfect for a long walk.

*****

Ike was the first one out of the door when the meeting ended. The old saying about the wheels of justice turning slow might be true, but someone should have come up with a phrase about how long it took to accomplish things when you had thirteen people on a City Council. It was a wonder anything ever got done.

That went against the grain with Ike. He considered things carefully before deciding, but he didn't let the process cripple him. Today was an example of how in the minority he was with that way of thinking. Some folks just seem hell-bent on talking a subject to death.

What concerned him now was that a member of the council he'd always found to be a reasonable, fair-minded man, and an ally, Mark Windom, didn't attend today's meeting. Ike took his phone from his pocket and placed a call to Mark.

It went straight to voice mail. "Hey Mark, it's Ike. Give me a call."

Having sat for nearly two hours, it felt good to move around, so he walked as he talked. As he slid the phone back into his pocket, he noticed Mark's truck parked on the street near the park entrance. Ike found that odd, so kept walking until he reached the truck.

It was empty. Why would Mark park here, and where would he have gone? Something wasn't right here. He couldn't imagine Mark had skipped the Council meeting without good reason. Would he be on the hiking trail? That didn't make sense either, but with no other possibility to consider at the moment, Ike decided it wouldn't hurt to walk down the trail and see if he spotted Mark.

*****

As Rylee walked, she considered her and Jack's findings. It was a given that someone erased the recordings for the entire twenty-four hours on the date of the hit-and-run. And whoever did it didn't breach the system.

But they certainly did cover their tracks. No evidence pointed the finger at any of the No Limits employees, yet that was the only pool of suspects. She knew that for a fact because no one could have broken the security without hitting one of what she liked to call *a tripwire*. When they designed the system, they made sure there was a landmine of tripwires and traps. She honestly didn't believe even the best hacker in the world could break the system.

So, if she stuck to that opinion, she had to rule out intrusion from the outside. Which only left the people working in the office.

She didn't like, nor could she come up with a reason for one of the people here to do such a thing. Then an image flashed in her mind of the empty storage card container in Brent's desk.

Surely Brent wouldn't have erased the data? But what if he did? A voice in her mind asked. What if something inconceivable happened? What if whoever killed that boy bribed Brent, offered him a bunch of money to erase the data?

What if he saw it and tried to blackmail the guilty party?

What if his accident was no accident at all?

She gave herself a headache with all the questions and reminded herself that her job was to figure out if there was a problem with the system or if they'd been hacked. It was starting to look like they had. From within. Which circled her back to her original question. Why?

Rylee needed someone to talk to but didn't know the people in the office well enough to start that type of conversation with one of them. And she didn't know anyone else in town except Matt and the Mayor, but she didn't want to involve Sharon. She pulled her phone from her pocket. Maybe she'd call Matt and see if he wanted to get together. She'd had no trouble conversing with him, and he seemed grounded.

But if she discussed it with him, it might put him in an awkward position. His father was on the City Council and close friends with the mayor. If she told Matt before she told them, they would probably be angry, and she didn't want that to happen or put Matt in an uncomfortable position.

She could always call her boss, Ian. No, she wasn't ready. All she had was speculation, and she needed proof.

But how? Letting her mind run through all the possibilities, she picked up the pace. Once she found the trailhead, she headed out, lost in thought and oblivious to everything except what was right in front of her.

Rylee hadn't walked far when she reached an overlook. It wasn't terribly high, but it was very rocky. A split-rail fence, obviously intended as a barrier keep people from getting too close to the edge sported a broken top railing.

She stepped closer and leaned out to look. A man lay below, and from the position of his body, the bloodstains on him and the rock beneath him, he was either unconscious or dead. A scream involuntarily ripped from her at the sight and she stumbled back.

"Hey!"

Rylee turned and glanced in the direction of the shout to see Ike Brickman running toward her. "Are you all right?" he slowed as he drew near.

"I am, but he's not," she pointed to the edge of the drop-off.

Ike walked to her and leaned out to check. "Dear God." He pulled out his phone to make a call. "Betty? Ike Brickman here. I need Joe. Now. And the emergency responders. Mark Windom is at the bottom of the overlook on the park trail just past the mile marker."

He paused, clearly listening to the person on the other end of the call, and glanced at Rylee. "What happened?"

"I don't know. I just found him. Tell them to hurry."

Ike did that, then turned his attention to Rylee as he pocketed his phone. "Did you see what happened?"

"No. I left the office to take a walk and clear my head, and when I got here, I realized the railing was broken, so I looked over and saw a man down below. Was that the police you were talking with? Are they sending help?"

"They are."

"Should I wait here in case someone wants to ask what happened?"

"That'd probably be a good idea."

"Okay." She looked away, not sure where to focus her attention.

"Are you all right?"

Rylee glanced at Ike and nodded. "Do you think he's alive? Should we try to climb down there?"

"I don't know that he is, and we'd need rope to get down there, so the best thing we can do is wait for help to arrive."

"Ok." Rylee crossed her arms tightly in front of her and hunched over into them, wishing she'd kept her coat with her. It was cooler under the shade of the trees, and the unease she felt at finding a dead body had her feeling a bit chilled.

"Here," Ike removed his jacket and held it out for her.

"No, you'll be cold."

"I grew up here. I think I'll survive it. And you're shivering. Put it on."

She slid her arms into the jacket as he held it. Once she had it on, he turned her to face him and zipped it up. "Thank you," Rylee was grateful. The inside of the jacket was warm from his body heat.

And it smelled good. Was that his scent? She wanted to bury her face in it. Rylee was suddenly ashamed. How could she have such thoughts when a man lay dead at the bottom of the overlook?

"How's it going with the internal investigation?" Ike asked.

"Confusing," she admitted.

"How so?"

Rather than answer, she asked a question of her own. "Did you know Brent? The man who died in the car accident?"

"Can't say I did, why?"

"Just curious."

"That's not a just curious question, Ms. Monroe."

How astute, she thought. She'd underestimated him. It dawned on her that perhaps he was someone she could talk to about her concerns and findings.

As she opened her mouth to speak, she heard sirens. "Looks like they're here," Ike said, took her arm, and escorted her off to one side. Within minutes, the place was swarming with firefighters in repelling gear, police, and paramedics.

An older man with a badge clipped to his belt strode over to her and Ike. "Joe Rogers, Miss. Chief of Police."

"Rylee Monroe, I work for No Limits."

"Yes, you took over for the fellow killed in the car accident."

"Yes, sir."

"So, what happened here?" Joe directed his question to Ike.

"I can only speak for myself, Joe. Mark didn't show up for the Council meeting. When it concluded, I walked outside and decided to stretch my legs before heading home. I saw his truck parked near the entrance of the park and wandered over to check it out. Nothing seemed out of place except what I already said, so I decided to hike the trail and see if I ran into him.

"I hadn't gone far when I heard a scream and ran to investigate. I found Ms. Monroe at the overlook, white as a ghost and shaking."

"Did you see what happened?" Joe asked her.

"No, sir," Rylee answered. "I saw the broken rail and leaned out to look and saw a man lying below. That's when I screamed. It wasn't but a few seconds before Mr. Brickman showed up and called you."

Joe nodded. "Thank you. Ike, why don't you escort Ms. Monroe out of here? I'd appreciate it if you met me at the station in about an hour to fill out a report."

"Sure," Ike agreed and glanced at Rylee. "How about we head to The Eatery and get some coffee. Joe, give me a call when you're ready for us."

"Will do."

Ike then turned to Rylee. "Shall we?"

There was no way for her to say no, and maybe this would give her a chance to talk to him about Brent and the hit-and-run. If she decided he was someone she could trust.

Chapter Eight

They walked in silence until they reached the entrance of the park. Rylee tried to get the vision of the man at the bottom of the overlook out of her mind, but couldn't stop thinking of it. Had he jumped? No, he wouldn't have broken the railing if he had planned to jump.

Or would he? Did he break the rail because he wanted to be found? No, that couldn't be it. How would he have broken it? Was he chased by a bear and fell? Or maybe he got into a fight and was pushed?

She knew she was focusing on what happened to keep from thinking about him lying there dead. She wondered how a person learned to forget seeing something like that. Rylee glanced up at Ike. Was he affected by what they saw?

He turned his head and looked down at her. His height made her feel short, even though she was five-seven. "Can I ask you a personal question, Mr. Brickman?"

"You can ask."

"You mean there's no guarantee you'll answer?"

"Exactly."

"Okay, I'll take my chances."

"Then ask away."

"Have you ever seen a dead person before today? And I don't mean at a funeral, but someone like–like that man in the park. Have you?"

"I have."

"And were you able to forget them? The way they looked. Did the image fade or does it stay with you forever?"

Ike stopped so suddenly she took another step before jerking to a halt. "You surprise me, Ms. Monroe."

"Why?"

"Because most people wouldn't even think twice about it, much less worry that the sight will be a lifelong companion."

"Oh god," she felt a little sick to her stomach at the idea that she'd always have that sight in her head.

"It'll get easier," he put his hand on her shoulder. "I promise."

"I hope you're right. Thank you for your honesty. Your son has that quality too, you know. He's honest and compassionate. I guess he learned that from you."

Rylee realized he'd had no way of knowing she'd met his son, so she revealed that bit of information. "I met your son."

"Which one?"

"Oh, I didn't know you had more than one. I met Matt one morning at The Eatery. He stopped in before heading for the park to do some drone piloting and search for hikers. I was glad to hear he found them."

"So was I."

"You must be proud of him. He's a nice man and apparently adept at flying—and not only drones. He did mention he also does cowboy stuff, but he didn't elaborate."

"I am proud of him, and while I wish he was as keen on ranching as flying, I can honestly say his skills are beneficial to everyone around here."

"How many children do you have, Mr. Brickman?"

"Three. Tom is the oldest, and he's a cowboy through and through. My daughter is Liz. She handles all the finances for the ranch."

"Sounds like a nice family. What about your wife? Does she work outside the home?"

"I don't have one of those."

"Oh, I'm sorry."

"Don't be."

Rylee didn't know what to make of that, so she changed the subject. "Is your family from here? Your parents, I mean."

"Yep, Pop is still going strong at nearly eighty, but prefers drone piloting and working with Matt more than ranching these days. He inherited the ranch from his father, who inherited it from his, and his before that."

"So, it's a multi-generational legacy?"

"Yes, it is."

"How wonderful. You and your family must feel like kindred to the land."

He paused and looked at her. "Yes, and I appreciate that insight. Most outsiders don't get it."

"Well, it's hard to understand what you haven't experienced, don't you think?"

It surprised her when he smiled and dazzled her a bit. Why couldn't she feel that rush of attraction for his son, Matt? Matt was handsome, sexy, and smart, and a lot closer to her age. Yet she didn't feel any spark with him.

His father was a different tale. But she sure as heck wasn't going to make a move on him, so she returned the smile and continued walking. "My family is originally from the mountains of North Carolina—well, father's folks, anyway. My mom's family is from Georgia. We lived in both states, but when I was fourteen, we moved to Florida."

"The Sunshine State."

Rylee chuckled. "Yes, it is that."

"You don't sound like you care for it much."

"It's a fine place, but Florida runs off tourism and is a transient state. There are small towns where everyone knows everyone, but they're dwindling, so the hometown feel is vanishing."

"Then why live there? You're a grown woman, you can go where you want."

"You want the polite answer or the honest one?"

"Honest. Always."

"Okay. Money. After college, I worked for the government for a few years. The money was okay, and the work was—well, it was exciting, but isolating because you could never talk about what you did. No Limits made me a great offer, so I took it and moved back to Florida. I love working for them and I want to retire before I'm fifty, so I was willing to stay in Florida where they're based."

"Then why move here?"

"Again, money." She looked up at him and smiled. "An insane amount, to be honest. I can retire in my forties if I don't screw things up here."

"And what will you do when you retire?"

"I don't have a clue. Learn to fly a drone, maybe ride a horse, or climb a mountain. Just live and hopefully not be stuck in a city somewhere."

"I'm with you on that." They stopped at the intersection and waited for traffic before crossing the road. "My turn," he said as they waited.

"For?"

"Asking a question."

"You can ask," she gave his words back to him.

His quick smirk told her he hadn't taken offense. "Was there video of Ethan's son getting run down?"

Rylee had to make a quick decision. Could she trust Ike Brickman? She sure hoped so. "I think there probably was."

"What does that mean?" he started to cross the street, but she reached for his arm, and he stopped.

"Let's not go to The Eatery yet. Let's go to my office," she suggested. "We'll have more privacy to talk."

Ike didn't argue, he just turned, and they headed toward No Limits, which was only half a block away. Neither of them spoke the rest of the way. When they entered, Sheila stood beside the reception desk where Rylee's secretary, Lynda, sat. Both women glanced in their direction, and Rylee noticed how their gazes went straight to Ike.

"I thought you were gone for the day." Lynda blushed and stammered.

"Mr. Brickman and I have some things to discuss. We'll be in my office. Please see we're not disturbed."

"Yes, of course."

Rylee headed straight for her office. "Can I offer you something to drink, Mr. Brickman?"

"No, I'm fine, thanks, and call me Ike."

"Thank you, sir. Please have a seat." She gestured to the sitting area.

Ike took a seat in one of the wing chairs that flanked the sofa, and Rylee settled on the sofa, angled toward him.

"Well?" he asked after a moment. "What did you mean by there probably was footage?"

"It means since our hardware and camera techs have assured me there was no problem with the cameras, video feed, computer or storage, the problem must be that either the data was never recorded, or it was removed."

"And you think it was removed?"

"Yes."

"Well, can't you prove someone removed it? That you were hacked?"

"But we weren't," she replied. "And that's the problem. I'd recognize a hack, and to be honest, our security is top notch. We're good at what we do, and it would take someone with tremendous skill to break past the security we have here."

"Then how could the data disappear?"

"By being erased, and not merely deleted. That would leave a bread crumb we could follow. No, whoever did it would have to possess serious skills at covering his or her tracks, and there just aren't that many people skilled enough. Not even some of the black hackers."

"Black hackers?"

"People set upon hurting, corrupting, or generally causing mayhem. Criminals. It makes no sense for this to be a black hack. There's nothing to gain, unless it was simply for a paycheck. But even if that was the case, someone needed a reason to have the data erased. If we can figure out the reason, maybe we can then figure out who did it."

"To erase all evidence of who killed Ethan's boy?"

"That's what I thought, too, then it dawned on me. To hire someone with the skills to pull this off would cost a lot, and I mean a crazy amount. Those people charge insane fees."

"Define insane."

"Hundreds of thousands."

"For one job?"

"For one job that can land you in prison if you get caught. But yes. So, we have to ask why would someone spend that kind of money to cover up a hit-and-run? Because they're a celebrity? Someone in politics? And even if they were, do you think they'd have any clue at all how to secure the services of a hacker? And at such short notice?"

Rylee shook her head. "No. There must be a bigger reason. There must be something someone wants to gain. Money or power or–" It hit her. "Or land. I remember reading something about some big developer wanting to build a wild west resort or something like that somewhere in Wyoming."

The expression that came on Ike's face told her she'd hit on something.

"These dang California billionaires," he grumbled. "They buy land like it's a game, try to blend in with the locals, and tell all their friends how great it is to live in such a paradise. Clear water and air, scenery that can take your breath away. Before you know it, some Realtor is knocking on your front door, offering you a silly amount of money and seeming genuinely shocked when you tell them to get off your land."

"What's a silly amount, if I may ask."

"Any amount, Ms. Monroe. That's my home. It's where five generations of my family have lived, worked, and died. I can't put a price on that."

"Please call me Rylee, and I understand. So, there is interest in buying land and developing it for a resort?"

"There's been talk, but the landowners are fighting it."

Rylee had a sudden sinking feeling in her stomach as the thought blossomed in her mind. "Was Ethan Caldwell and the man we found at the park landowners who didn't want the resort to be built?"

"Why?" Ike asked.

"We need to look at today's footage. I remember seeing the location of the cameras when I was studying the location on the flight here. There's a camera that shows the park entrance and one that looks out over the small valley from the overlook."

"Do you think you'll find something that will help the police figure out what happened to Mark?"

"I hope so. Come on, let's go to the hub of this operation."

She led him into what they called the control center. Rylee took a seat in front of a monitor and keyed in a sequence on the keyboard. A second later, the sight of the park entrance displayed on the monitor.

"Pull up a chair,"

Ike slid a chair over next to her. "What are we watching?"

"A live stream."

"Is there any way to view the video from earlier?"

"What time?"

Ike hesitated for a moment. His brows drew together, and he pinched his bottom lip between his thumb and index finger. "Three hours ago. That's about when everyone showed up for the meeting."

Rylee accessed the time frame Ike gave her, and they fast-forwarded until Ike spoke up. "That's his truck."

They watched as the vehicle came to a stop and a man got out. He glanced around, pulled his phone from his pocket, and made a call. Rylee made note of the time code. His conversation lasted barely five seconds.

Then he pocketed his phone, scanned around, and headed for the walking trail.

She fast-forwarded the video, but they didn't see anyone park beside Mark's truck, or anyone go down the trail until they saw Rylee crossing the grass in that direction.

"I'll make a copy of this and give it to Chief Rogers," she volunteered.

"What good would it do? There's nothing on it."

"Isn't there?" She swiveled her chair to face him. "It shows him making a call."

"Your point?"

"That maybe whoever he made that call to is involved. At least the Chief will have the time and can have the phone records subpoenaed, since this is an incident that ended in someone's death."

"Smart thinking. Let's do that."

"On it." She got up and went to a cabinet on the side of the room, fetched a thumb drive, and returned to her seat. Once the data was downloaded to the thumb drive, she removed it and offered it to Ike.

"No, it stays in your hands until we give it to Joe."

"Okay, do you want to do that now?"

"I sure do."

"Then let's go."

They left the building and headed on foot across town. Rylee looked up at him after a few minutes of silence. "If the Caldwell boy and this man Mark Windom were both killed, and both families were against the resort, do you think this could be a way for someone to frighten people into agreeing to the development?"

"It's possible," Ike answer. "But not smart."

"Why is that?"

"Because people around here don't scare easy, and if you start a war with us, we're going to fight back."

"I understand, but what if people keep dying? How long will you let it go on until you at least agree to sit down and discuss it?"

Ike stopped and gazed at her. "If we find evidence that leads us to believe that's what is happening, I'll call for a meeting myself."

"If we find evidence?"

"Isn't that what you're supposed to do?"

His expression told her that's what he expected of her. She just didn't know how to tell him she was out of ideas about how to accomplish that.

Chapter Nine

Rylee was exhausted by the time her clock chimed to let her know it was time to start the day. She spent most of the last week glued to her computer at work during the day, and every night logged into the No Limits system, trying time after time to figure out if there was a clue how the data went missing.

No matter how many times she looked, she always ended up at the same place—convinced that someone at No Limits intentionally erased the data. The problem with that theory is that only one person had the skills. Brent.

Rylee's mind kept going back to the empty packaging for the memory card. She calculated the amount of storage needed for a day's video. The card wouldn't hold all of it. So, she calculated how much storage it would require for an hour's worth of video. There was more than enough room for that.

Had Brent copied the footage to a memory card, then erased the entire day? If so, to what end? Rylee lay back and stared at the ceiling. After ten minutes, she blew out a breath, threw back the covers and rose from the bed.

Half an hour later, showered and dressed, she went into the kitchen, started the coffee, then fetched her phone. It was still early, but she got the impression Matt Brickman was an early riser, so she took a chance and called him.

"Good morning," he answered on the second ring. "I was planning on calling you this morning."

"Oh?"

"Yeah, I have a free day, and I thought I'd offer to teach you to pilot a drone. If you're still interested, and can take the time."

"Are you kidding?" Rylee was not only eager to learn but also wanted to talk to Matt about the missing data. She couldn't ask Ike what she wanted to ask Matt. "When and where?"

"Why don't I pick you up in–half an hour?"

"I'll be ready. Do you want the address?"

"I know where you live."

"Oh," she was a bit surprised, but tried not to let that be evident. "Then I'll see you in half an hour."

While she waited, she fixed herself a cup of coffee and sat at the bar separating the kitchen from the living area, and opened her laptop. Her first task was to email her boss, asking if he knew if Brent's place had been cleared out, and his belongings sent to his family. She also asked for permission to go there and see if she found anything out of the ordinary. She made a point to say that if the request sounded like she suspected something was amiss; he was right, and she'd welcome the chance to speak to him about it.

Rylee hoped that when she voiced her suspicions, he would help her either refute or validate them. She was eager to get to the truth of this missing data, regardless of who was responsible.

Her next email was to Lynda at work, to say she would work from remote until Monday, but was available via text or phone call. After that, Rylee checked her email, replied to those requiring a response, and wrote an email to her brother, Rayce, telling him about the beauty of Wyoming and about the handsome cowboy-slash-pilot who was going to teach her how to pilot a drone.

As she finished the email, there was a knock on her door. Rylee hurried to answer and found Matt standing on her front stoop, smiling. "You ready?"

"I am," she replied. "Come in while I grab my phone."

She glanced back over her shoulder at him as she turned and headed back toward the kitchen. "Do you think I'll need a coat?"

"This is Wyoming, you should always dress in layers."

"Excellent advice. Give me two minutes. Help yourself to coffee if you're interested."

"Thanks."

Rylee dashed to her room, grabbed a long sleeve button-up shirt and put it on top of her long-sleeved knit top, then grabbed a lined jacket she'd picked up at a store in town and headed back to the kitchen.

"Good coffee," Matt commented, and took another drink from the cup he held.

"Want to take it with you? I have some thermal cups."

"Sure."

"Here, let me have it." She took his cup into the kitchen, transferred the contents to a thermal cup with a lid, and then glanced his way. "Top it off?"

"Sure."

Rylee filled the cup, screwed on the lid, and handed it to him. "Okay, I'm ready."

"Then let's do it."

"I'm with you."

The big pickup truck he indicated had writing on the door. Brickman Ranch. She climbed into the passenger seat and buckled up. "So, where are we headed?"

Matt started the truck and glanced at her. "The ranch."

"Okay." She was curious about his family's ranch. Even in just the short time she'd been here, she heard the name mentioned in stores and restaurants by men and women alike.

"What're you thinking?" Matt asked.

"What makes you ask?"

"You pulled together your eyebrows like you were thinking about something serious."

Rylee smiled. "You're observant. I was thinking about your family. I've heard the name Brickman a lot since I've been here."

"And? What's your impression of my family based on what you've heard?"

"That you're all well-respected, a little feared by some other landowners, trusted by most, and the men in your family–you included–are a subject of fantasy for many women around here."

Matt laughed. "A subject of fantasy? That's a good one. Nightmare is more like it."

"Why would you say that?"

He shrugged. "Let's just say that the men in this family might be lucky at a lot of things, but love isn't one of them."

"No? You've never been in love?"

"Hell yeah, a hundred times, but none of it real."

"Well, what about your brother? Tom, right?"

"Yeah. Tom is in love. With the land. If ever a man was born for life on a ranch, it was Tom."

"So, he's a rancher? Not a cowboy?"

"He has a cowboy's soul and a rancher's brain. His love of both is too big for any woman to compete with, although Dad would love one of us to get married and give him some grandkids. So would Pop and Gigi, my grandparents."

"I met them one afternoon while taking a lunch break. They were sitting outside the Eatery on the patio, dining with the mayor and her husband. The mayor saw me and yelled for me to come meet them."

"And?"

"And they're wonderful. Friendly and kind. And wow, the way they look at one another." Rylee didn't consider herself high on the romantic scale, but the way the Brickman's looked at each other made her yearn for what they had. Real, enduring love and an attraction that hadn't dimmed.

"Yeah, I guess they sucked that particular well dry, and the rest of us are just S.O.L."

Rylee knew that feeling. "My parents are that way. It sure can make you feel like a failure in the relationship game."

"Tell me about it. So, does that mean you're not in love either?"

"Until this moment, no." Rylee was awestruck as they cleared the town, and she got a good look at the landscape before her. "But now... Oh, my god, Matt. This place is breath-taking."

"Yes, it sure is," he agreed. "So, I guess we might both be in love with the same things."

"You mean work, reaching goals, and this paradise?"

"That's about it."

"And for now, that's enough." Rylee smiled at him and changed the subject to what had occupied her mind since the day she arrived in Wyoming. "You know, I couldn't sleep last night for thinking about what happened to Ethan Caldwell's son and the mystery of the missing data."

"You still don't have any answers?"

"I have a lot more questions than answers."

"Like what?"

"Well, to begin with—and I know it probably goes without saying, but I'll ask you to treat this as confidential?"

"Sure."

"Okay, first, I have found no evidence of a security breach, which tells me our system is sound. And I also feel the need to affirm that I'm not claiming that to absolve the company I work for from any liability or responsibility. I examined that system like a freaking electron microscope, looking for anything suspicious or something that would suggest an abnormality in function or fluctuations in speed—in anything the least bit out of the ordinary. There simply isn't anything indicative of a breach, or even an attempted breach."

"Look, I'm not into all that next level computer stuff, but I know data—footage, can't be erased without leaving markers. So, was there footage to begin with? Or did someone turn things off for that day?"

"Good questions and ones I've asked. And you're right about leaving markers. For the most part. There are people clever enough to fool the machine and make it appear the data was never there to begin with. But I don't know that's what happened here. Still…"

"You think it might be?"

"Yes," she admitted, what she didn't want to believe. "And the reason I do is so small, that maybe I'm just creating a straw to grab because I'm empty-handed."

"What's the straw?"

Rylee considered for a moment. Once the words were out, she couldn't take them back. And she could be wrong. Maybe Matt's reaction to her theory could help her decide.

"The straw is I found an empty container for a memory card in Brent's desk drawer. Someone had removed the card and left the wrapper in the drawer. I thought that was odd, but at the time I found it, it was just an anomaly that merited little consideration.

"Until I unlocked the door and let my mind go into *what if* mode."

"What's that?"

"You know, coming up with possible scenarios."

"Like?"

"Like what if someone paid to have the footage removed? They didn't need the entire day, only a few seconds, but if they took just what they needed, it would draw more scrutiny. They wanted it to appear the data simply vanished because of faulty security or some glitch in the code."

"Okay, so what if someone paid to have the footage erased?"

"Well, if someone did, the easier thing would be to copy the data onto a storage card. It's so small you could drop it in your shirt pocket, and no one would ever notice."

"You're talking about it like it was someone on the inside."

"I know."

Matt glanced over at her, and there was no longer a smile on his face. "You think that guy who was killed in the car accident is responsible?"

Rylee had to be completely honest, or she couldn't ask the same of him. "I don't know, but it's all that makes sense right now. Let's say it's true, and he took the footage and basically sold it to someone. Who? The guy who killed the Caldwell boy? If so, then the murderer isn't some run-of-the-mill cowboy or grocery store manager. It would cost hundreds of thousands of dollars to buy that level of hack and make it worth the risk. So, who has that kind of money around here?"

Matt's frown vanished, and his laugh shocked her. "What's so funny about that? Matt, stop laughing. It's not funny."

It took him a second, but he was still smiling when he answered. "Who has that kind of money? Rylee, you can go into any restaurant in town, throw a rock in any direction, and hit at least one billionaire. You've probably read it, but it didn't sink in. This area is one of the highest concentration of wealth in this country. The owners and CEOs of some of the biggest conglomerates and corporations in the world call this place home. So, who could afford it? Throw a rock."

Rylee considered what he said and nodded. "All right, so this couldn't be someone upset about Caldwell not being in favor of the wild west resort some developer wants to build?"

"Hell no. The people who don't want that can buy that developer out with their pocket change."

It was almost embarrassing. Rylee had let her imagination get the best of her, and had not only failed to find how and why the system was breached but also cooked up a conspiracy that failed the first obstacle. Matt's reaction had shown her that she'd rushed to a conclusion, rather than following the breadcrumbs one at a time.

She wouldn't make that mistake again.

Chapter Ten

Ike stood on the front porch, watching as Matt tutored Rylee on flying a drone. They'd been out all morning. Matt and Tom took her riding, and then Matt started showing her how to pilot. Ike noticed Matt had chosen an older model, and not one of the higher priced commercial drones he used for business.

She seemed to be taking to it. Ike couldn't help but wonder if she was taking to Matt as well. As he watched, his parents drove up in their fancy ATV they liked to drive to and from the main house.

"They're still at it?" his mother asked as she got out of the vehicle.

"Looks like it." Ike stepped down from the porch. "What you got there, Mom?"

"Lunch." She lifted a large basket out of the back of the ATV and added. "There are two more that need to be brought in."

"You didn't have to cook for us." Ike accepted the basket, and one more she handed him.

"Well, you do have company, Ike. And I know Bear's a heck of a cook, but this is his day off, so I thought I'd help. Unless, of course, you'd rather I took all this back home."

"Heck, no." He moved out of her reach.

She laughed and made a grab for one of the baskets. "You got that other one, hon?"

"Yep." Asa lifted the largest of the baskets.

"Then let's take it in and get it ready." Ike's mother, Georgia, led the way, stopping at the steps to call out. "Matt? Five minutes till lunch. You and Rylee come get washed up."

"She talks to them like they're kids," Ike said to his father.

"Hell, they are, son." Asa smiled and glanced at Matt and Rylee. "You think he's taken with her?"

"Don't know. I wasn't even aware they were friends until he showed up with her this morning and said he was going to show her the ranch and teach her to fly a drone."

"Well, she's a pretty woman, that's for sure, and smart as they come."

"I reckon so." Ike wasn't about to admit that he considered Rylee attractive. To stop further conversation on the topic, he headed inside, leaving his father to follow.

"Ike?" Georgia called out. "Call Tom and tell him to come to the house."

"Yes, ma'am." Ike wouldn't think to argue with his mother. She'd obviously gone to a lot of trouble to cook a meal, so the least they could do was sit down and enjoy what she'd prepared.

As soon as he placed the baskets on the kitchen counter, he fished his phone out of his pocket and called Tom. "Hey, son. Your grandmother fixed lunch, so come on to the house. Yep, right now. Okay."

He looked at his mother. "He'll be here in five minutes."

"Good. Okay, let's get all this to the table."

Just then, Matt and Rylee entered through the kitchen door. Ike and Asa both turned at the same time. "There's my boy," Asa said with a grin. "How're the drone piloting lessons going?"

"She's a natural," Matt replied.

"I bet she is," Asa replied, and then addressed Rylee. "How are you today, Ms. Rylee?"

"Better now that I see your handsome face," Rylee replied and laughed as Asa enveloped her in a big hug.

"Hey," Matt greeted Ike and his grandfather, then turned to Georgia. "Hey, Gigi."

Matt's greeting brought a smile to Georgia's face, and she turned and opened her arms. "Come give me a hug."

"With pleasure." Matt lifted her off the floor with his hug and returned her to her feet with her laughing. She glanced at Rylee and smiled. "I'm glad to see you again, Rylee."

"I'm happy to see you, Mrs. Brickman. What can I do to help?"

"Well, you and Matt wash up and I'll put you to work."

"Yes, ma'am." Rylee hurried to the sink, and just as she turned on the faucet, Matt stepped up beside her, bumped her with his hip, and laughed when she flicked water from her fingers at him.

Ike watched, and to his surprise, found himself a little envious. Matt and Rylee seemed so at ease with one another, like they'd known each other for a long time. Were they attracted to one another, or simply contented to be friends?

And why should it matter to him either way? He was, after all, way too old for her. Sometimes he missed being young. Today was one of those days, but he wouldn't dwell on it.

"Pop, grab a stack of dishes and I'll get the silverware." He said.

"Let me do that," Rylee said.

"You're a guest, you don't have to–"

She cut him off. "I'd like to help, and it'll give me a minute to catch up with Mrs. Georgia."

Ike looked at his mother and she smiled. "You men can wait on the front porch. We'll have it on the table in two shakes."

"Never argue with Gigi," Matt said, and headed out of the kitchen with Asa two steps behind.

"Go on, Ike. We promise we won't talk about you behind your back," Georgia said.

"I don't," Rylee said. Then she and Georgia looked at one another and laughed.

Ike had no idea what to think or say, so he just headed out of the room. Once he left, Georgia looked at Rylee. "So, you and Matt?"

Rylee shook her head and stared unloading containers from the baskets. "Just friends. God knows he's hot as a match, but there's just not any heat if you know what I mean." She laughed. "What am I saying? Of course, you know. I've seen how you and Mr. Brickman look at one another."

"And that's what you want, isn't it?"

"Isn't that what everyone wants? Happily ever after, enduring love and passion?"

"It sure is. I was halfway hoping you were on your way to finding it with Matt." She paused in what she was doing to add. "But you can never have too many good friends."

"Amen to that," Rylee agreed. "And goodness knows I was blessed the day I met you and Mr. Brickman. I told Matt how seeing the two of you together made me think of my Mom and Dad."

"Do you miss them?"

"I do, but I text all the time, and once I get things squared away at work, I'll take some time to pay them a visit. I wish you could meet them."

"And I'd love to." She went to an enormous walk-in pantry and came out with a serving cart. "Okay, let's put everything on the cart, and set up in the dining room."

"Yes, ma'am." Rylee hurried to comply, and in just a few minutes they had the table set and the table laden with food.

"You go get the men, and I'll get the iced tea and a pitcher of water."

"On it!" Rylee headed outside and found Ike on the front porch with one hip hitched on the porch railing as he watched his father fly the drone while Matt and Tom stood by, watching and talking.

She said nothing, and just watched for a moment, wondering what Georgia would say if she knew there was only one Brickman Rylee was interested in? Ike. She wouldn't admit it aloud, but she accepted it as a fact. She had a thing for Ike Brickman.

As if sensing her presence, he glanced her way, and her breath caught when their gaze connected. Rylee was positive she'd never had this type of reaction to a man. She had once claimed she wanted to know what it felt like to be completely spellbound by a man. Now she almost wished she didn't know, because she didn't think she stood a chance with him, and that didn't make her happy at all.

"Everything's ready," she sauntered over to him. "You have it all, don't you, Mr. Brickman? This place? It's like something out of a dream. I'm sure there's work, probably a lot. Even so, in every direction you look, you see something magnificent. And you have a wonderful family who obviously love one another. What more could a man want?"

"There's a thing or two," he said, and the way he said it had that breath-catching thing happening again. What the heck? She needed to get a grip.

"Well, I hope you get it," she said, and looked away before she could be swept away again in dreaming.

"Not much chance of that, Rylee." He stood and took a step closer. At that moment, she realized the attraction wasn't a one-way street. That made her happy, so much it emboldened her.

"There's always a chance, Mr. Brickman. It really depends on how bad you want it."

"You think that's all it'd take? Wanting it?"

"Well, at some point, you have to act. All want and no action doesn't get you where you want to go, does it?"

"Not as rule."

"Then maybe you need to get in motion and go after what you want."

He gazed at her for a long moment before looking away with a bit of a snort. "I'll give it some thought."

With that, he walked by her and called for the rest of the family to come in to eat. She watched and smiled. Ike Brickman liked her. He might be reluctant to act on the attraction, but now that she realized she wasn't the only one interested, she would follow her own advice.

Only not in front of his entire family.

With a smile and a bit of a bounce in her step, she headed inside.

"Well, don't you look like the cat who licked the cream?" Georgia said when Rylee stepped into the dining room.

"Do I?" Rylee started fiddling with the napkins and silverware, straightening, or adjusting, just to avoid Georgia's gaze.

Just then, Ike walked in. He stopped in the doorway with his gaze on Rylee, then noticed his mother and smiled. "It sure looks good, Mom."

"Doesn't it? Rylee helped me set the table. It's nice to have company, isn't it?"

"Yes, ma'am." He cut a glance at Rylee and just as quickly looked away.

"Wow, this looks great." Ike's oldest son, Tom, said as he stepped in, followed by Matt and Asa. "Gigi, you outdid yourself." He hurried over and lifted Georgia into a hug.

"You're just angling for an extra big piece of chocolate cake," she laughed when he set her back down.

"Chocolate cake?" he waggled his eyebrows, then looked in Rylee's direction. "Hey there, beautiful. You ready for another riding lesson?"

"Absolutely." She agreed enthusiastically. Until today, she'd never ridden a horse and even though her rear felt a little sensitive from all the ungraceful bouncing, she was eager to give it another try.

"Well, tell me when, and we'll do it."

"Thanks, Tom. You're the best."

"Don't I know it?" He nudged Matt out of the way. "Here you go, Rylee. Sit beside me."

She smiled, winked at Matt, and let Tom pull out her chair. The next hour passed with a lot of laughter and everyone sharing memories. It was easy to see the love between the people present, and Rylee appreciated being included in the moment.

When the meal ended, Matt walked over and leaned down to speak to her. "I'm going to call and have the helicopter made ready, and I'll fly you to the national park for a drone lesson."

"Is that permitted? And where do you land a helicopter?" She rose from her chair.

"There's a landing pad just outside the park," Ike answered the question, and Asa took up the narrative. "And thanks to the gift the ranch made of a dozen ATVs to help with search and rescue, they're always willing to let us borrow one."

Rylee looked around and then at Ike. "This is an amazing family. Thank you for allowing me to share a meal with you. Matt, make the call, but give me twenty minutes. I want to help clean up."

"No, you won't," Georgia argued. "You're a guest."

"I'd rather be a friend." Rylee meant what she said. There wasn't a person here she didn't like. "And friends help."

"Then get your butt in gear," Georgia said. "Let's get all the plates stacked on the serving cart first, and we'll come back for the rest."

"Yes, ma'am." Rylee turned and didn't realize Ike was standing behind her. She would have collided with him had he not taken hold of her upper arms and stopped her forward momentum.

"Sorry," she looked up at him.

"No apology needed. It was nice having you here, Rylee. You're welcome anytime."

"Be careful, Mr. Brickman. You keep talking like that, and I'm going to start thinking you're a friend."

The smile he gave her said a lot more than words, as did the slight squeeze he gave her arms before releasing her. "Well, since friends do dishes, I'll leave you to it."

"Oh, no you don't," Georgia retorted. "You're going to help Rylee load up that cart while your dad, Tom and I haul these serving dishes to the kitchen."

Tom opened his mouth and spoke four words before he was cut off. "Gigi, I have to–"

"Get busy. You eat, you help. Or…"

"No, don't say it." He pleaded dramatically.

"Or I take the rest of the cake home with me."

"Out of the way, Pop, I'm earning cake."

It didn't take long with everyone pitching in, and it reminded Rylee of dinners with her family and everyone working together. She missed her family, and today helped fill a bit of that emptiness. Rylee hoped she'd have more opportunities like today, but for the first time in her professional career, felt insecure.

She needed to figure out what happened to that missing data, or her company would suffer a hit in their reputation, which meant they could also suffer a financial hit. Rylee didn't want to be responsible for that. Her biggest problem was that all indicators pointed her in a direction she didn't want to go.

Namely, it was an inside job, and the man responsible was now dead.

Chapter Eleven

Ike had just opened the refrigerator door when Matt and Rylee entered through the back door. "Dad, I need a favor," Matt dove right in without taking time to say hello. "The County Rescue just called, and I need to go out and help find a missing child. Can you give Rylee a ride home?"

"Sure son, go find that child, and be safe."

"Just like my father taught me," Matt replied, and turned to Rylee. "Sorry to dump you on Dad."

"Don't be. You're doing something important. I hope you find the missing child. Text me later and let me know?"

"Sure." Matt paused long enough to give her a hug that lifted her off her feet and a quick kiss. "Okay, I'm outta here. Goodnight, Dad."

"G'Night, son." Ike waited until Matt left, then addressed Rylee. "Hungry?"

She smiled at him. "Starved."

He might not have recognized the double entendre if it were not for her smile. Ike leaned back against the kitchen counter. "Rylee, we need to get some things squared away."

"Okay. Before, during or after we eat?"

That statement had Ike thinking he was dumber than he realized, but she sounded like her interest was food. "You're hungry?"

She laughed and walked over to stand in front of him, with less than a foot between them. "I said I was starved, didn't that give it away?"

Hell fire. The last thing Ike wanted to do was admit he thought she was insinuating she was starved for something besides a meal. It surprised him that she didn't wait for a reply. "I'm sorry, Mr. Brickman. I'm awful at flirting I guess, but I was trying because–well, you know, because I think you're hot and it's been a while since–well, never mind. The point is, if you're not interested, you can just say so."

"Do you know how old I am?"

Again, she laughed and dang if it didn't sound sexier than before. "Sir, I want to have sex, not get married. You can still do that, can't you? At your advanced age and all."

He almost took offense, then realized she was teasing him. "You've got a mouth on you, don't you?"

"And you're good at evading a question, aren't you?"

Ike couldn't help but smile. "Some things are better kept to yourself."

"Shame," she said and turned to open the refrigerator. "There are a ton of leftovers in here. Want me to fix up a couple of plates?"

"Shouldn't I be asking you that?"

"Oh, I'm sorry. Did I overstep?" She stepped back from the refrigerator and let the door close.

Ike hated the crestfallen expression on her face. He hadn't meant to hurt or offend her. He'd meant to suggest he should serve her since it was his house. Damn it. She had him off balance, and he didn't like it. Ike was accustomed to being in control, and she somehow stripped his control away with no effort at all. Or so it seemed.

"No, I just don't want you to think you have to serve me."

"Oh, I don't," she smiled and opened the refrigerator again. "How about we do this together? I'll take everything out and put it on the counter and you get plates."

It relieved him she'd bounced back so quickly. "Sounds like a plan."

Within minutes, they had plates filled, warming in the microwave, while Ike poured glasses of ice water. "We have tea if you'd prefer that," he offered.

"Sweet?"

"No."

"Thanks, I'll stick with water."

"We have wine."

"I hate wine."

"You hate wine?" That stopped him in his tracks. He'd never met anyone who hated wine. "What's to hate?"

"The way it tastes. Not just bad, but awful. Like someone took all the good out of the grape and left this sour, bitter, turn your mouth inside out… stuff."

Ike laughed. "Well, I reckon it's an acquired taste."

"And like so many other things in life, I never acquired it." The microwave dinged, and she opened the door. "Oh crap, that's hot," she snatched her hand back from the plate.

"Gloves," he said, and opened a drawer, pulled out two thick oven gloves and slid them on.

She stepped aside so he could remove the plates. Ike carried them to the table, placed one at the head of the table, and the other at the space beside it.

Rylee took the seat on the side and lifted her water glass when he was seated. "Thanks for your hospitality, Mr. Brickman. I appreciate the meal and the company."

"It's my pleasure, and you were supposed to stop calling me, Mr. Brickman."

"Thank you, Ike."

"You're welcome. Mind if I ask a personal question?"

"I don't know, ask me and find out."

"Fair enough. Are you involved with Matt?"

She sat back in her seat. "We're becoming friends, if that's what you mean."

"No, it's not."

"Oh, well, then the answer is no. I think he and I were meant to be friends."

"I see."

She went back to eating, then stopped. "Would it bother you if I was involved with Matt? Or Tom?"

Ike considered the question, and almost lied, but that wasn't something he made a habit of, so he answered honestly. "I think it might."

"Why?"

Just then, the phone rang. "Excuse me," he rose and picked up the cordless phone from the kitchen counter. "Hello? Hey Joe, everything all right?" Ike looked at Rylee as he listened to Joe. "Okay, thanks, Joe. I'll find out."

He put the phone back into its cradle and returned to the table. "That was Joe Rogers."

"The Police Chief?"

"Yes."

"Is everything okay?"

"No, Rylee, I don't think it is. He wants you to volunteer to come to the station in the morning and be fingerprinted."

She pushed back from the table. "Why?"

"Because there was a print recovered from Mark's body. On the face of his watch. The coroner says it appears he might have been in a fight before he fell, or was pushed."

"And they think it was me?"

"They're ruling out the possibility it could be."

The pleasant, relaxed woman of a few minutes ago vanished, and in her place was one with steel in her eyes. "Then have them check with the FBI. My prints are on file."

That shocked him. "Why would they have your fingerprints?"

"Because I worked for the government."

"Oh. Well, I—well, hell." Ike got up to fetch the phone and called Joe. "Hey, Joe, listen, Ms. Monroe said you can check with the FBI. Her prints are on file." He glanced at Rylee as he listened. "Yes, she worked for the government."

A few seconds later, he ended the call. "Will do. Good night, Joe."

"So," he looked at her after he replaced the phone in its cradle. "You look mad."

"Disappointed," she said in a voice devoid of warmth.

"Because?"

"Because I'm being regarded as a suspect, when all I did was find the body."

"But no one knows that, do they? Not for certain."

Her face lost some of its rigidity, and for a few moments she sat there staring at him. He'd be willing to bet she wasn't looking at him. Her eyes were just pointed in his direction. Her expression said she was somewhere else.

"You're right," she finally spoke. "The video didn't show anyone follow him into the park. In fact, there was no one who entered the trail other than me. So naturally, I would have to be considered a person of interest. Nevertheless, when Chief Rogers gets a copy of my fingerprints, he'll know it wasn't me who pushed that man."

"I'm glad to hear that."

This time when Rylee stared at him, he saw a woman who was either worried or afraid. "Can I talk to you about something Mr.—sorry, Ike?"

"I don't see why not."

She nodded. "I'm going to need your word that you won't repeat any of what I'm about to say."

"I don't know if I can do that."

"Okay," she said, and picked up her plate. "Do you have a garbage disposal or a compost bucket?"

"Closed bucket under the sink," he replied.

She made short order of emptying her plate, rinsing, and putting it and her utensils into the dish washer. "I'm ready to go home now, if you're still willing to give me a ride."

"Rylee, I–"

"No, it's okay, Mr. Brickman. I understand." She moved to the kitchen door to take her jacket from the coat rack.

"No, I don't think you do. If you tell me something I feel needs to be reported to the authorities, I'll be honor bound to report it, which would break confidentially."

"Oh!" Rylee stopped in the midst of putting on her coat, then frowned and continued. "Well, you're right. Still, I've taken up enough of your time."

"Fine." Ike marched over to the coat rack and snatched his coat off. He shoved his arms into the sleeves, shrugged it onto his shoulders and crammed his hat on his head. He then opened the door. "After you."

Rylee opened her mouth, then closed it and went outside. She reached the bottom of the steps and stopped. "Wow," she breathed as she looked up. "Now that's a sky."

Ike stopped beside her. "Florida has a lot of sky."

"It does," she agreed. "But there's so much light it takes away from the view of the night sky. Except maybe on some beaches that don't allow development. Then it's magnificent. I just don't get to the beach much."

"Why?"

"I guess I'm too focused on work."

"That's a shame," he remarked. "A beautiful young woman like yourself should enjoy her youth, not let life slip by you for the sake of a job."

"Says the man who owns – she glanced at him. What? Three hundred thousand acres or so?"

"Something like that."

"I imagine there's work involved in building and tending a ranch this big."

"There is. The trick is knowing how to balance work and play."

"Really?" She smiled, and he knew before she spoke again, he'd walked into a trap. "Then why don't we stop at that place Matt mentioned, some saloon just at the edge of town with live music?"

"The Barn?" he walked beside her to his truck.

"Yes, I think that's what he said it was called. He said I should get out and do some boot scootin', but not to get suckered in by a cute cowboy if one asked me if I was interested in knocking boots, whatever that means.

Ike shook his head. "It means have sex." He opened the truck door for her.

Rylee laughed as she climbed in. "Of course, that makes sense. You people have some interesting ways of phrasing things, don't you?"

"I reckon."

For the first few minutes, they were silent. Rylee stared out of the window. "I still want to talk to you, Ike."

"In confidence?"

"Yes."

"Fine."

"Fine? Okay, thank you."

"So, what is it?"

Rylee gathered her thoughts. "As my grandmother used to say, the Reader's Digest Condensed version is like this. The missing footage that might have shown Donny Caldwell's death was deliberately erased. And it had to be an inside job. Our security is next to impossible to break."

Ike glanced over at her. "Okay, we'll circle back to the inside job, but first, no security is unbreachable."

"I hate to be argumentative and don't want to appear boastful, but the good old government of the USA says my algorithm is titanium. There are maybe a handful of hackers in the world who could break the encryption, and only half of those who could do it before the system detected the attempt and shut down."

"So that's what you did for the government?"

Rylee smiled. "That and hacked."

Ike was surprised. She looked like a beautiful young woman barely out of college, full of ambition and enthusiasm. Not a world-class hacker who worked for the government. That old saying was true. Looks could be deceiving.

"Well, color me surprised, Rylee. So, let's go back to your statement that it was an inside job. What brought you to that conclusion?"

"Because if the system can't be hacked from outside, the only way to take the data and leave no trace is to be on the inside, someone who knows the system inside and out, and how to be a ghost in the machine."

"Do you know who that someone is?"

She glanced at him and bit her bottom lip for a moment as if deciding whether to answer. Ike got the impression this was the moment she was deciding if she could trust him. He hoped she decided she could, and it surprised him that it mattered. He barely knew her.

"I think so. I think it was Brent Corsa."

"The man who died in the car crash?"

"Yes."

"What makes you think that?"

Rylee told him about the empty memory card case, and what the No Limits employees had told her about Brent's behavior before his death. "It's out of character and a big change in his routine, which is even more significant."

"Why is that?"

"Because he's like me, only worse."

"Meaning?"

This time, the silence stretched long enough that he felt something was wrong. "Rylee?"

"Brent is–was a highly functional autistic, obsessive about his work. He could get caught up in a project and lose track of time to the point he'd go a full twenty-four hours without stopping."

"And you're that way?"

"I'm not autistic, but I am mildly OCD. I've learned how to control it so it can't control me."

"So, you and he were a lot alike?"

"In some ways. Obsessive, driven and prone to be rigid with deadlines. I just have a better memory."

"He didn't?"

"Oh, no. He did. But I have something similar to hyperthymesia."

"What's that?"

"Extremely good memory."

"Like what they once called photographic memory?"

"Something like that. Hyperthymesia is also referred to as highly superior autobiographic memory or HSAM. And people with HSAM can recall details of experiences with extreme accuracy. Some researchers have noted that HSAM people also share characteristics with people who are OCD, which I have been diagnosed. I have not been formally diagnosed with HSAM, and I don't believe I have it. I can remember almost every line of code I've read, but I can't tell you what I ate yesterday. It puzzled doctors for years. When I left home to go to college, I refused to go through any more tests or assessments.

"And that's not important. The point is, people with certain conditions, most notably autism, are extremely unlikely to vary their routines. So, for him to be responsible for the missing data, something extraordinary would have had to happen to compel him to do it."

Ike cut her a look. "Such as?"

"I don't know. I've been trying to figure that out. The only thing I can come up with is that he probably would do it to save someone he loved."

"Like the fellow he lived with?"

"Dennis? Yes, most definitely. He and Dennis have been together since they were teenagers. Dennis was the one person in the world Brent truly trusted. He would have done anything for Dennis."

"So, are you telling me you think someone threatened Dennis to get Brent to erase the data?"

"Yes."

"Okay, so taking a step back. Why does that make the memory card important?"

"Because I think Brent made a copy of it, and if I can find it, maybe it will show who ran Donny Caldwell down."

Ike wasn't ready to admit it aloud, but he was impressed with all the thought Rylee had put into this. "And how do you think you can accomplish that?"

"I don't know yet, but I'll figure it out."

"I just bet you will, and I hope you'll tell me when you do."

"I might."

"Might?"

"Trust has to be earned, Ike. If you earn mine, then I'll tell you."

"Fair enough."

"Oh wow, look at all those stars," she changed the subject. "Is there a major difference in the sky from one season to the next?"

The rest of the drive passed with them talking about the sky, the landscape, the temperatures, and her asking a thousand questions. Ike had never met anyone so curious, or so enthralled with the world around her.

When they reached The Barn, the parking lot was full, which was to be expected for a Friday night. "You sure you want to go in?"

"Yes, indeed," she said and grinned.

"Okay then," Ike got out of the truck and headed around to open her door. But by he rounded the front of the truck, she was already standing there.

The noise and smell hit him with near tangible force when he opened the door. Ike wasn't a fan of loud music or cologne, and there was a preponderance of both in the bar. He also didn't much care for the number of people watching him cross the bar with Rylee. By tomorrow, a lot of people in Brickton would be talking about him carrying on with some gal young enough to be his daughter.

He almost turned around and left, but just then Rylee, who was in the lead, glanced over her shoulder, smiled, and turned enough to grab his hand and pull him along behind her.

Oh, shit. Ike let her tug him along to a small, two-person table. She peeled off her jacket, climbed onto one of the bar stools, and patted the other, which was close to her own. Then she leaned in close. "Good grief. Do you have any idea how many people are staring at us?"

"I'm pretty sure I do."

Her smile was a flavor he hadn't witnessed until now, and if he had to describe it, he'd call it wicked. That turned out to be a fair assessment, based on what she said next. "Then why don't we do like the old song and give them something to talk about?"

"Like wh–"

He never got the rest of the word out before she climbed onto his lap, straddled his legs, wound her arms around his neck and kissed him. "Come on, Ike, you can do better than that," she said against his lips.

"Screw it," he grumbled, wrapped one arm around her body, tangled his free hand in her hair, and kissed her. At first, she tensed as if surprised, but then made a little noise he could barely discern in all the racket, and gave herself over to the kiss.

People say your first kiss is the one you never forget. He might once have believed that, but not anymore. This was the kiss he'd never forget. The way she surrendered, then savaged, her breasts pressed against his chest, making him aware she didn't wear a bra, and her nipples were hard. Then there was the action going on below her waist, a rub and roll that was causing way more reaction south of his belt than he dreamed was possible in a public place like this.

Ike realized with sudden clarity that she made him feel young. It was intoxicating. So much so that he gave in to the moment. It wasn't until someone tapped his shoulder that the kiss ended. Rylee smiled, but didn't move from his lap, and the middle-aged gentleman spoke.

"Well, I reckon hell's done froze over. I never expected to see you here, Ike."

"Life's full of surprises, Roy."

"Indeed, it is," Rylee chimed up, slid off his lap, taking his hand as she did. "Hi, I'm Rylee and I'm stealing Ike from you. He's going to teach me to knock boots. Have a good night."

Ike saw the look that came on Roy's face, but refused to react to it. Once they were on the dancefloor, Rylee looked around at all the dancing couples plastered together as the band played a slow crooning tune. She mimicked what they did, forcing Ike to hold her close.

123

"It's boot scoot," he said as she pressed the side of her face on his chest.

"I know." She laughed. "What the hell. Teach me to boot scoot or knock boots. I bet I'll love both."

"You're going to be trouble, aren't you?" he asked, hating how much he enjoyed moving her around the dance floor, feeling her pressed against him.

"I'm sure going to try Ike," she looked up at him. "And you know, I *am* an OCD gal so..."

Ike just shook his head. He'd have to keep his wits about him around Rylee, or he was going to be tempted to show her how Wyoming men knocked boots.

Chapter Twelve

Rylee checked her watch as she slowed. She'd run almost daily since she arrived in Brickton, and was finally overcoming the elevation. It would take her a while longer to get back to where it was, but at least she was making progress.

It was the only thing she was making progress on. Since her Friday night non-date with Ike, she'd flip-flopped from thinking about their kiss to the missing data. It made her ashamed that she was far more obsessed with the kiss.

She allowed herself the weekend to daydream about the handsome Wyoming rancher, vowing to focus solely on the missing data starting on Monday. She'd spent every day since then going through the system, and Brent's office with the equivalent of a microscope, examining every line of code, every command, and every inch of his physical space.

And now, on Wednesday, was still empty-handed. There had to be something she was missing. But what? She stopped at the intersection of Main and Broad Street and waited for the light to change to cross the road.

As she stood there, she gazed up at the web camera mounted on the tall pole beside the streetlight. It towered over the light and was protected by a sturdy glass cage. She knew its coverage area and looked out, trying to imagine the footage it was capturing. As she did, it occurred to her that this camera just might have recorded at least a partial view of the Caldwell boy's hit-and-run.

Why hadn't she realized that before? She felt like a dunce.

Eager to find out if she was right, she broke into a run as soon as the traffic light changed. She ran straight to the office, tossed a "hey" at Lynda, who sat at the reception desk, and hurried to her office. It took only a few minutes to access the files from the event and the correct camera. Rylee wasn't sure about the time, so started at 9 pm and quickly forwarded through the footage.

At eleven-eighteen, something caught her eye, and she slowed the replay. Her heart sped up as she saw headlights appear two blocks down as a vehicle stopped before turning onto Billings Street. The clarity wasn't great thanks to the distance from the camera, but when the lights turned the corner onto Billings Street, she could see what looked like someone walking down the sidewalk.

Whoever the person was, started running, but wasn't fast enough. The vehicle swerved onto the sidewalk and hit the runner, who went flying up and then landed on the street. Rylee put her hand to her mouth, covering the "oh shit" she muttered. She watched closely as the vehicle turned off Billings and onto Sweetwater Street. As it did, she realized it was a truck. She couldn't tell the make or model, or how old, only that it was dark and what appeared to be a man wearing a baseball cap was driving.

For the next half hour, Rylee worked to enhance the video, but there was only so much she could do with the software on hand. Still, it was something, so she copied the footage onto a memory card and picked up the phone to call Chief Rogers.

The man who answered said the Chief was out and wouldn't be back until the next day. She asked the officer to leave a message, asking the Chief to call her, and then hung up. Now what?

The first thing that popped into her mind was to call Ike. But she couldn't involve him. Could she? Maybe he would know how to contact the Chief. They were friends. But then so was Sharon, and being the mayor, she deserved to know what Rylee had found.

Rylee called Sharon on her cell phone, and the call was answered on the second ring. "Hey there, Rylee. What's up?"

"Are you busy?"

"I'm about to step into a meeting, but I'll be free in an hour. What's up?"

"I have something I need to show you."

"About Donny's death?"

"Yes."

"Meet me at my office in an hour."

"Okay, see you then."

Rylee stuck the memory card in her wallet, replaced the wallet in her messenger bag along with her phone and laptop, grabbed her jacket and the bag she'd put her work clothes in when she changed to run. She could use the executive bathroom at the office, but would rather go home and get clean.

So, that's what she did. It took her less than half an hour to shower and dressed. After that, she took a seat at the bar in her kitchen and plugged the memory card into her laptop.

Her phone rang, and she snatched it up from the bar. Matt's photo showed on the screen. "Hey," she answered. "What's up?"

"Girl, what did you do to my dad?"

"Pardon?"

"Friday night. I've heard from at least half a dozen people that Dad was at The Barn, carousing and making out with some young woman. And the man was whistling this morning. Whistling."

Rylee hadn't considered how quickly gossip moved in small towns, or that people would have paid attention. But then she hadn't considered that Ike was well known, something of a pillar of the community and a man of some importance in this part of the state.

"Uh, well, I wouldn't call it making out. And that might not play a role in him whistling."

"So, it did happen?"

"Sort of."

"You're a wicked woman, Rylee Monroe."

"Not really. Besides, you're not interested, and a girl gets lonely and—and well, he's hot, you know."

"Oh, you didn't need to say that. That's my dad."

"Whatever. Are you mad at me?"

"Hell no. We've been trying to get him to think about dating for a long time. I just always figured it would be with someone his own age."

"So, you think I'm too young?"

"No, but some folks do."

"And does your dad know about those folks?"

"Oh yeah, Pop was knocking on the door before breakfast Saturday morning to tell us about the people he'd already talked to."

"I bet Ike was furious."

"He was, and he wasn't. To be honest, I think it gave his ego a boost."

Rylee chuckled. "Men and their egos. Well, I'm glad he wasn't mad. Is that why you called?"

"No, I was thinking about something you said, and I went back through some drone footage and found something I want to show you, but you can't let anyone know I have it."

"That sounds mysterious—and a little ominous. Can I ask what it is?"

"I think I caught part of your friend's accident. I was filming for the county that day, looking for potential problems with the road. Pop was with me. I don't know how I missed it, but when I went back and viewed all the footage, I saw something. I'm going to take it to Chief Rogers, but wanted to show you first. Are you going to be home tonight?"

"Yes, I am. Come for dinner. I'll get takeout from The Eatery."

"Is that your way of saying you don't cook?"

"Oh, I cook, you just wouldn't want to eat it."

"Then call it in and I'll pick it up on my way. Would six work for you?"

"Perfect. See you then."

Rylee ended the call and checked the time. She had plenty of time to walk to Sharon's office. After putting her laptop and phone back into the messenger bag, she looped the strap over her shoulder and left the condo.

She thought about the conversation with Matt. What could he have seen that had him willing to give up his evening and drive all the way into town to show her? She couldn't guess, so put that out of her mind.

Other thoughts occupied her during the walk, thoughts of Ike and their evening. Rylee had genuinely enjoyed their time together. After a few beers, Ike loosened up, and she saw a side of him she hadn't seen before. He knew how to flirt, and he was sexy doing it.

She couldn't remember ever enjoying an evening so much, and when he dropped her off at the condo, she said as much. To her surprise, he echoed the sentiment and squeezed her hand. Funny how that gesture was as significant as a kiss.

It was times like these she wished she had a girlfriend to talk with, but so far, the one friend she'd made was Matt, and he sure wasn't a girl. And he was Ike's son, which made it difficult to talk to him about having the hots for his dad.

She dismissed those thoughts as she drew near the Town Hall where Sharon's office was located. Sharon was waiting in her office, and stood the moment her secretary showed Rylee in. "Oh, you don't look happy." She rounded the desk, took Rylee's arm, and guided her over to the sitting area.

"Call me frustrated," Rylee said, and sat on the couch. "Today when I returned from running, I realized that one of the other cameras in town might have caught what happened to the Caldwell boy, so I checked and sure enough, it did."

"So, you know who the driver is?" Sharon sat beside Rylee.

"No. I tried to get up with Chief Rogers, but he's not in, so I thought it would be okay if I showed you. But if I'm breaking protocol–"

"Not at all. Show me."

Rylee removed her laptop from the messenger bag, plugged in the memory card, and played the footage. She noted Sharon's reactions. How one of her hands went to her chest and the other latched onto Rylee's arm. "Oh, dear god. We have to find out who that man is. Can we do that?"

"Not with the software we have available. We're not set up to enhance video."

"Which means?"

"It means you need specialized software that has algorithms that can analyze multiple neighboring frames and choose the best pixels to reconstruct a higher resolution version of the original."

"I have no idea what you just said."

"I need specialized software."

"Okay, do you know what kind of software does that?"

"Yes, ma'am."

"And how much does it cost?"

"About thirty-five hundred."

Sharon's hand moved from Rylee's arm. She stood and paced the floor for a minute, then looked at Rylee. "I'd love to tell you the town will spring for the cost of the software and your time, since this is outside our contract, but I don't think I'd be able to talk the town council into it, and I'm sure your boss won't pay for it."

"There's one way to find out." Rylee pulled out her phone and called her boss. It took no convincing. He said for her to do what she felt they needed to do, because No Limits was dedicated to helping the people of Brickton find out who was responsible for the death of the young man.

Rylee thanked him and ended the call. "We're fine. He said we'd pay and do the work at no charge to you.

"Well, color me surprised. What now?" Sharon asked.

"Now I need you to go with me to No Limits to watch the footage and witness me make a copy for Chief Rogers, to verify that what you saw is what is on the memory card we'll give him. I don't want there to be any doubt. Then I'll take my copy, purchase the software, and start enhancing the segment of the video that shows the truck and the man wearing the ball cap."

"Okay, do you know how long it will take?"

"Honestly, no. And I won't start until the Chief has seen the footage."

"That's fair. Do you want to go to your office now?"

"Yes, ma'am."

"Would you please quit calling me ma'am?" Sharon grabbed her purse and jacket. "I'd like to think we've become friends."

"I do think of you that way, but this is business, and I don't want to overstep." She said as she closed the laptop.

"You're not honey, trust me, I'd tell you if you were."

"Well, thank you," Rylee finished packing up her messenger bag and stood.

They left the building and crossed the street. As they strolled, Sharon started a conversation. "So, I hear you and Ike had quite an evening at The Barn on Friday."

Rylee considered the statement and realized Sharon was fishing for details. "Well, I don't know about Mr. Brickman, but I had a good time."

"That's what I hear."

"Oh?"

"Yes indeed. Something about you sitting on his lap, making out?"

"Oh, we weren't making out."

"You weren't?"

"No, we were just kissing."

"From what I heard, it was some kiss."

"Well, then you heard right," Rylee said and smiled. "It most definitely was."

"And?" Sharon asked.

"And now all the guys his age think he's one hell of a stud, attracting the attention of a young woman that way, and having her all over him in public. And the women who might not have noticed him before, sure will now."

"What makes you think it will change women's perception of him?"

"Because any women there who were watching now know that Mr. Ike Brickman has moves on and off the dancefloor."

Sharon laughed. "So, you were doing community service?"

"Hell no," Rylee answer. "That was all for me."

Sharon laughed again, and this time Rylee did as well. It felt good to admit that to someone, and in such a way that Sharon couldn't know if she was being serious. Not that she was ashamed of having an infatuation with Ike Brickman. She feared that maybe he didn't feel the same. After all, she hadn't heard from him since Friday.

Wouldn't a man who was interested have picked up a phone and called? Suddenly, her good mood vanished, and insecurity reared its head. Rylee told herself to put her personal issues aside. Right now, she needed to focus on helping to identify who killed Donny Caldwell. Her crush on Ike Brickman could wait.

Chapter Thirteen

Rylee had the table set and was standing at the bar, working on the video she'd downloaded. Sharon contacted Chief Rogers so they could show him the footage. He told them to save the original copy, but to proceed with the enhancement. Rylee purchased the software on the company credit card as soon as she returned home, installed it on her laptop and spent an hour familiarizing herself with the user interface.

Now she had the footage loaded and was working to see how much she could zoom in on the man in the truck. A knock on her door prompted her to close the laptop and hurry to answer.

"Food delivery." Matt grinned and held up two takeout bags, one in each hand.

"Thanks for picking it up." Rylee stepped aside for him to enter. "I have the table set. What do you want to drink?"

"Do you have beer?"

"Yes, I bought Rolling Thunder, Honey Drip, and regular old Bud."

"I'll take a Bud."

"Okay, coming up. Just put everything on the table."

Rylee took a beer from the refrigerator for him. "Glass or bottle?"

"Bottle is fine."

She grabbed her glass of water and carried both to the dining area. "You're not having one?" Matt asked as she handed him the beer.

"I don't drink."

"Ever?"

"No. Never developed a taste for alcohol."

"I don't think I ever met anyone who didn't drink."

"Well, now you have. So, do you want to eat or talk about why we're here?"

"Both. You have a laptop?"

Rylee snorted. "Move the place settings to one side and I'll set the laptop between us."

While Matt took care of the table, she fetched her laptop from the bar. As soon as she put the laptop on the table, Matt pulled a memory card from his shirt pocket and handed it to her.

"Sit," she gestured to a chair and sat in the one beside him. When she opened her laptop, he gazed at the screen.

"What's that?"

Rylee hadn't planned on discussing this with Matt, but suddenly realized she couldn't expect him to trust her if she didn't return the favor. "I was coming back from a run today and stopped at the corner of Main and Broad, and it hit me. The camera on the corner might have captured what happened to Donny Caldwell. It'd be from a considerable distance, so the resolution would suck, but there was a chance it could at least show the make of the vehicle.

"So, I hurried back to the office and searched the footage, and sure enough there was something." She backed up the footage to where the truck turned onto Main Street.

Matt watched and muttered "son of a bitch," when the truck struck the boy, and his body went sailing. "Keep watching," Rylee said.

She froze the video when the truck made a turn off Main Street. "Does anything about this truck or driver look familiar?"

"There are a hundred trucks that look the same in this town or surrounding area, and a hundred men who wear ball caps." He continued to stare at the footage. "Wait, back it up."

She did and started the replay. Just as the truck turned the corner, Matt said, "Stop."

Rylee stopped it again. "Can you zoom in?" He asked.

"Already tried that. The imagine is too distorted to see the driver clearly."

"I wanted to see what was on the rear window."

Rylee looked at the frozen image and quickly set about to zoom in on the window of the truck. Sure enough, there was an emblem or sticker of some sort. "Do you recognize that?"

"I might. Where's the card I gave you?"

She pulled it from her pocket. "Plug it in," Matt said.

Rylee did as she directed, and in moments was watching an aerial view of a winding road through mountainous terrain. "What's this?"

"Like I told you earlier, I was filming for the county the day your co-worker was in the accident. We were looking for potential problems with the road. Pop was with me. I don't know how I missed it, but when I went back and viewed all the footage, I saw something."

"What?"

"Go to four minutes and nine seconds."

Rylee did as instructed and watched a car traveling at what seemed a reckless speed from the way it floated from one side of its lane to the other. Two seconds later, a black truck appeared, bearing down on the car.

"Freeze that," Matt said. "And zoom in."

Rylee did, and one glimpse at the screen had her turning her attention to Matt. "That's the same sticker, isn't it?"

"I think so. Also, another thing that's strange is the truck has no tag."

Rylee slowly fast forwarded, and managed to see the rear of the truck before the drone's path took it over the vehicles. "What if this is the same truck?"

"What if it is?" he asked. "What if that truck is the reason your friend died? Something had to force him to drive off the side of the road in the one spot where the guardrail was missing a section."

"We have to take all this to Chief Rogers."

"I agree. In the morning. He won't be there tonight, so we might as well eat."

"You're right," she stood, moved the laptop to the bar, and then unloaded the takeout bags sitting on the table.

"I'm glad you shared that with me," she said as she started loading her plate.

"And I appreciate you sharing the footage you found with me. Between us, I think we have at least a starting point for Chief Rogers."

"I agree." She lifted her fork, then lowered it to her plate. "But I still don't understand why someone would kill Donny Caldwell?"

"Or your friend?"

"Actually, I have a theory about that."

"Which is?"

"That Brent erased the footage, but he made a copy and was going to sell it to someone. Maybe that's why he was on the road that day, to meet whoever it was and turn over the evidence, but instead he ended up getting killed."

"That's reaching, don't you think?"

"Maybe, but it would sure explain things."

"Yeah, it would. You should tell the Chief your theory."

"Maybe." She picked up her fork to resume eating. "Can I ask you a personal question?"

"Sure, fire away."

"Does your dad know you're gay?"

Matt cut her a look that answered her question. "What makes you ask something like that?"

"Just curious."

"Okay, but why? What would make you think I'm gay?"

"I have eyes, you know. I've seen how women and men look at you. You ignore the women and try not to notice the men. I watched my older brother go through that for years before he finally realized that being gay didn't make him less of a person, or a deviant."

"Your brother is gay?"

"He is."

"What does he do?"

"He's a Marine. A big bad ass Marine."

"And he's okay with his sexual orientation?"

"Yes, why shouldn't he be? Our choices of sexual partners, or who we fall in love with, isn't all that define us, is it? We're born the way we are, and like my mother always said, if God didn't intend us to be this way, we wouldn't have been born like this. And you know, my mother is probably one of the smartest people I've ever known."

"I think I might like your mother."

"I'm sure you would, and she'd love you. But back to my question, why haven't you ever told your dad?"

"Have you met my dad?" he paused and gave her a side-eye look. "Oh yeah, I forgot you've not only met him, but you've also made out like teenagers in a crowded bar with him."

Rylee smiled. "I'm not in the least ashamed of that. And I don't think he'd care, Matt. I spent an evening with him and asked him about his family, and it's clear he loves and is proud of you."

"He wouldn't be able to handle it."

"I think you're selling him short, but it's your business, so I won't say anything. But I appreciate your honesty."

"You're welcome. Do you think you can do the same?"

"Be honest? Of course."

"Okay, are you just messing around with my dad because you're bored or are you really interested in him?"

Rylee stopped eating and turned her chair slightly so that she was facing him. "Matt, I don't get involved much. Not men or women. And no, I'm not bi, I just don't have many friends, and I have never been in love. I don't meet many men I'm attracted to, and I've always thought maybe God made me to be alone.

"Then I met your dad, and it was like a switch that'd been turned off my whole life suddenly turned on. So yes, I am genuinely interested, but I'm not in love with him. I don't even know him. But I'd like to have time to."

"I think you'd be good for him." Matt got up, picked up his empty bottle, and headed for the kitchen. "Mind if I have another?"

"Have all you want. If you have too many, I have a guest room you can use."

"I have a better idea," he stopped.

"What?"

"There's a honky tonk just at the edge of town, The Wildcatter. Let's go dancing."

"On Wednesday night?"

"Yeah, the place is hopping on Wednesdays."

"You like to dance?" She didn't know why that surprised her, but it did.

"Love it. You game?"

"Are you kidding? Let me finish eating and I'm in."

"Cool." Matt headed on into the kitchen and returned with another beer. It took them less than fifteen minutes to finish eating and clean things up, then they headed out.

"I'll drive," she offered.

"I can drive."

"I know, but if I drive, you can drink."

"Good point, you drive."

It took less than five minutes to get to The Wildcatter, and the parking lot was packed. She found a place to park and got out of the vehicle. Matt met her at the front of the car. "So, I have to ask," she said. "Am I your date or wingman?"

"For this place, my date. Is that a problem?"

"Are you kidding? My creds in this place will be sky high if I'm seen with you."

"How do you figure that?"

"Remind me to tell you to look in a mirror."

Matt laughed. "Right back at'cha girl." He offered his hand. "Let's do this."

Rylee grinned and clasped his hand. Sure enough, the moment they entered, heads turned in their direction. Rylee had not realized how many single women there were in Brickton, or how many women there were out cruising for some male companionship or excitement.

The way women were staring at Matt reminded her of hungry cats looking at one bowl of cream. There sure wasn't enough for everyone, which meant there was always the possibility of a cat fight.

She'd almost pay to see that. As long as she wasn't the one getting scratched. "Wow, it's like being out with a movie star," she leaned in toward him to tease. "Do we play it cool or give them something to talk about?"

"What do you think?" he grinned as they reached the edge of the dance floor.

"That's my guy," she returned the smile and then laughed as he swung her into his arms.

It didn't take long to discover that he had something in common with his father, aside from good looks. He had moves. Matt was one heck of a fine dancer, and more than one woman tried to cut in on them.

It delighted Rylee he refused their offers. She was also secretly thrilled about the number of men who tried to cut in.

They danced for nearly an hour before the band played a slow tune.

"Do you have any idea how many people in this place want to be in my shoes?" she asked as he pulled her close.

"Not as many as would like to shove me out of the way."

"Hardly," she argued. "I wish you could meet my brother, Rayce. I think you and he would hit it off—at least as friends. He's a lot of fun to be around, a real outdoors kind of guy and one heck of a decent person."

"Then you should invite him to visit, and we'll take him out to the ranch for some riding, fishing and flying."

"Oh, he'd love that. Thank you."

"What are friends for?"

It hit her at that moment that he had become her friend. Rylee genuinely liked Matt and enjoyed being with him. There weren't many people she could say that about. "You know, your family is really something."

"How so?"

"You're all so easy to like and admire."

"That's probably one of the nicest things anyone's ever said to me."

"Well, it won't be the last as–" At that moment, time did a quick freeze-frame, and she realized what he couldn't because his back was turned. A man with a full-face mask stood at the edge of the dance floor pulling a gun from his belt.

Fear spiked fast and hard. "No!" Rylee screamed as the man raised the weapon. Terrified Matt would be hurt, she spun him around, putting her back to the man and not thinking of the danger, only of protecting Matt.

It was the oddest thing. She felt something slam into her back a split-second before the sound of the gunshot brought a moment of silence to the bar. The impact drove her into Matt, who wrapped his arms around her and pulled her to the floor.

That's when the pain kicked in and all the air went out of her lungs. Rylee gasped and wheezed, feeling like she couldn't draw a breath. "Rylee, stay with me," Matt said, and then yelled. "Call for an ambulance. Now!"

The place was in pandemonium, with people screaming and fighting to get out of the door. Rylee was barely aware of what was going on. All her focus was on trying to draw a breath.

A voice yelled that an ambulance was on the way. Rylee heard it and recognized she was injured, but oddly, wasn't afraid. Why was that? Hadn't she been shot?

"Matt," she rasped.

"I'm with you, Rylee. He cradled her in his arms. "You stay with me, okay? Stay with me."

"I'm..." she felt something strange, like her energy was just seeping out, stealing her of all strength. "I'm...". The rest of the words wouldn't come. She saw darkness creeping in her periphery, darkness that grew quickly until she felt herself fade into nothingness.

Chapter Fourteen

Matt jumped up from his chair when his father stepped into the waiting room. "Thank God you're okay," Ike grabbed Matt in a tight hug.

"She saved me, Dad," Matt wiped at his eyes. "I could have been killed, were it not for Rylee and now...". He shook his head and turned away.

Ike put a hand on his son's shoulder and led him back to the chairs lined against the wall. "Tell me what happened?"

Matt sat and leaned forward, propping his elbows on his legs, and clasping his hands between his knees. "We were dancing, having a good time, and suddenly she grabbed my arms and spun us around so that we swapped positions. A split-second later I heard the gunshot, and she sort of lurched forward like someone had shoved her hard, and when I caught her, I felt something wet. "

He paused and looked at Ike. "Now she's in surgery and I can't get anyone to tell me anything because I'm not family."

Ike nodded. "Well, I reckon we better try to get up with the people she works for and find out how to get in touch with her family."

"I don't know any of them, and I'm betting they're not at work at this time of the night."

"You're right. We'll have to wait until morning to get in touch with them."

Matt leaned back and rubbed his hands over his face. "If we could get her phone, maybe we could get her parent's phone number."

"Don't you reckon she'd have it password protected?"

"Shit. You're right. So, what do we do?"

"Wait." Ike said and leaned back.

"That's it?"

"That's it," Ike clapped his hand on Matt's knee. "And pray."

"That's all I have been doing since I got here."

"Then keep it up."

Matt leaned back and closed his eyes. Ike watched him for a moment. If it weren't for Rylee Monroe, he might not be sitting here beside his son. Rylee saved Matt, and her bravery and caring were being rewarded with—what? Would she survive?

Ike didn't want to consider the possibility that she might die. Not simply because he was indebted to her for saving his son, but because, whether he wanted to admit it, he liked her.

He was troubled, not only over Rylee's condition. Why would someone try to shoot Matt? There seemed to be a lot of people getting killed in Brickton, and for the life of him, he couldn't figure out why. He'd thought about Rylee's suggestion that perhaps it had to do with the proposed theme resort, but dismissed that.

There were more than enough people in this county with the financial means to stop any such development. So, what else could prompt the crimes being committed? Ike leaned back, closed his eyes, and tried to think. What did the Caldwell family, Mark Windom, Brent Corsa from No Limits and Matt, have in common?

Trying to come up with an answer to that question claimed his mind, and he literally jerked when a voice spoke up. "Is there someone here for Ms. Monroe?"

"We are," Matt answered.

"Are you family?" The man clad in what Ike assumed was a surgical outfit asked.

"No, but–"

"We will be." Ike interrupted, and despite hating lies in any form, let one slide right between his lips. "She's my... my fiancé."

"Oh, I didn't realize, Mister...?"

"Brickman," Ike stood and offered his hand. "Ike Brickman."

The doctor shook Ike's hand. "She came through the surgery. The bullet passed through a lung and nicked an artery. She's lucky to be alive.

"Will she recover?"

"She will. She's young and strong, and I expect her to make a full recovery. We will keep her a few days, however."

"Can we see her?"

"She's in recovery, but as soon as she's conscious, I'll have someone come get you."

"Thank you, doctor, you have my gratitude."

"And mine," Matt added.

"Just doing my job, but I appreciate the sentiment. Now, if you'll excuse me, I'll get back to our patient."

"Of course," Ike agreed.

Neither he nor Matt spoke until the doctor left, then Matt turned to him. "Your fiancé? Seriously?"

"You already said you weren't family, and someone needs to get in and see her, and make sure she's getting proper care."

"I didn't think of that. Still. You lied."

"Friend, fiancé—I used the wrong label."

Matt grinned. "Yeah, whatever you say, Dad.

Ike grunted and reclaimed his seat. What the heck had prompted him to say that? Was it because he wanted to make sure she was getting good care, or was there more to it? He wasn't ready to tackle those questions. It'd been a long time since he'd been with a woman he liked and had fun being around, and even longer since he'd met someone he found interesting and appealing.

Rylee Monroe fit all that, despite being younger. It occurred to him he didn't know her age. "So, how old is she anyway?"

"Four years older than Tom."

"Thirty-seven?"

"Yep," Matt answered and then added, "And since you're fifty-three, you're not old enough to be her father in case that's what you were worried about."

"Who said I was worried?"

Matt snorted and leaned back in his seat. "Dad, if you're interested in Rylee, it's fine with the rest of us. Aside from Liz, who hasn't met her, the rest of us like Rylee. And that old crap about age difference is just that. Old crap. There shouldn't be an age limit on liking someone."

"I appreciate that, Matt, but sixteen years is a significant difference in age."

"So? If it doesn't matter to you or her, who gives a hoot what other people think? Didn't you teach me to be true to myself and follow my conscience rather than the opinion of someone else?"

It surprised Ike to hear those words returned to him. He realized that while he often wondered if his words as a father had an impact; it was now clear those words were not wasted breath at all. His son had not just paid attention, but remembered.

"Thanks for reminding me, Matt. You're a good son."

"So?"

"So what?"

"Are you interested in Rylee?"

Ike felt the immediate need to hide from the question or lie and asked himself why. Was he ashamed he was interested in Rylee or afraid Matt would consider him a foolish old man?

"I think she'd make a fine friend."

"The mayor and her husband make fine friends, Dad. What you need is someone who's more than just a friend to have lunch with in town."

"Is that so? And what about you? What do you need?"

"The same thing."

"Then maybe you should look at Ms. Monroe."

"She's not my type. And don't turn this around. We're talking about you. I know she likes you and I think maybe you like her. And like Pop always says, we have a limited number of days. Don't waste any of them being unhappy if you have a chance at happiness."

"He's a smart man."

"Yes, he is."

"Then maybe we both should take his advice. Maybe you need to find someone to share your time with."

"I'm looking, Dad, just haven't found the right person yet."

"You will, son." Ike clapped Matt on the knee. "You will."

"I hope," Matt replied.

The hours ticked by slowly. When the sky outside started to lighten, Matt stood and stretched. "You want some coffee? I'll go find some."

"I wouldn't say no to it."

"Okay, I'll be back."

Ike watched him leave, then rose and went to stand in front of the window, looking out over the parking lot and into the distance. Funny how life worked. Here, the town faced people getting murdered, and the person who was supposed to figure out who was doing it ended up almost getting killed saving his son.

Which circled him right back to the question. Why? Why would someone want to hurt Matt? Or was the goal to hurt him? Was Matt a target intended to inflict the pain that Ethan Caldwell now suffered? And if so, who had he wronged so badly that they'd want to kill his son?

"Mr. Brickman?" A female voice from behind made him turn around.

The nurse standing just inside the door smiled. "Your fiancé is awake if you'd like to see her."

"Yes, ma'am, thank you." He started across the room, but stopped. "My son went in search of coffee. Could someone check back here in a few minutes to let him know where I am?"

"Of course, this way, sir."

Ike followed the nurse down the hall to a room. She opened the door, speaking as she entered. "Miss Monroe? Your fiancé is here."

Ike wished she hadn't announced that, but the damage was done, so he gritted his teeth and followed her into the room. One glance at the hospital bed, and he forgot all about his embarrassment and quickly skirted around the nurse.

"Jesus, Rylee."

"I imagine he might have played a hand in this. I am alive, after all." Her voice was weak, and from the pallor of her skin and her expression, she appeared in pain.

Ike picked her hand up from the bed and held it between his. Her skin was cold, and that bothered him. "Should she be this cold? Do you want to get the doctor?"

"She's fine, Mr. Brickman," the nurse smiled and indicated the bank of monitors. "Although, your presence seems to have raised her blood pressure a bit."

"Is that bad?"

"In this instance, no." She glanced at Rylee. "Are you in pain?"

"Some, but it's manageable."

"Well, if it becomes unmanageable, use your call button."

"I will, thank you, Alice, you're so kind."

"Just doing my job, sugar. Now, I'll leave you in what appears to be the capable hands of your handsome fiancé."

"Thank you."

Ike watched the nurse leave, then turned his head to notice Rylee watching him. " Fiancé?"

He shrugged slightly. "They'll only let family in, and since you don't have any here, I had to come up with something."

"That's okay, Ike. I appreciate you being here. Matt's okay, right?"

"He's fine, thanks to you. You saved his life, Rylee. I'm in your debt."

"No, you're not."

"You could have died."

"But I didn't, and it was the right thing to do."

"Your parents must be some kind of good to have raised you to feel that way."

"They're the best."

"Then why don't we call them? I'll be glad to pay for them to come here, and they can stay at your condo or the ranch if they'd rather. We have plenty of–"

"No."

"Pardon?" Ike was shocked. "You don't want them to know?"

"No."

"Can I ask why?"

"No."

"Rylee–"

"No, Ike. You can't know and you can't call them, and we can't talk about my parents."

A beeper started sounding on one of the monitors and alarmed him. In two seconds, the nurse, Alice, rushed in. "What in the world are you people doing in here to shoot her blood pressure through the roof?"

This time, it was Rylee who lied, and that surprised Ike. "Well, you know when you have a hunk like this hovering over you, it's hard not to get worked up."

Alice laughed, and Ike forced a smile. "Well, I think it's time for your hunk to go and you to get some rest." She looked at Ike. "You can come back in the morning."

"Can you take my number just in case?"

"Of course, just stop by the nurse's station. Oh, and your son is in the waiting room."

"Thank you." Ike felt a bit on the spot with the nurse there, and wasn't sure how Rylee would react, but he tried to keep his cool and play the role he'd assigned himself. He leaned over and kissed her lightly. "Sleep well, sweetheart."

"Be safe going home," she replied.

"I will. I'll see you in the morning."

"Can't wait."

Ike turned and headed out of the room, recognizing that now he had another question with no answer. Why was Rylee so against him notifying her parents on what had happened? That seemed out of character. Or was it? He barely knew the woman.

And yet he had labeled himself her fiancé. What the hell was he thinking?

Chapter Fifteen

"Since you were the one to negotiate with Mr. Grant of No Limits on the original contract, I think you should be the one to call him."

Ike suppressed the urge to remind Sharon that the only reason he'd done the negotiating was that no one else would step up, but everyone was pushing to get the camera program underway. Instead, he nodded and rose from his seat.

"Are you not going to finish your coffee?"

"I've had plenty. I'll let you know what I find out. I'm going to head over to see Joe before I go to the hospital."

"Matt was lucky," Sharon said. "I've spoken with several people who were there, and they all say if she hadn't gotten in front of Matt, he'd have caught a bullet to the chest. I think that makes her something of a hero."

"She has my gratitude and that of my family, Sharon. We'll be in her debt for her act of heroism."

"I figured as much. I hope you find out how to contact her family." She swallowed the last of her coffee and stood. "And between you and me, I find it odd that she doesn't want anyone to contact her folks."

Ike shrugged, not wanting to speculate on Rylee's reasons. "I'll be talking to you. Have a good day and tell Earl I'll see him at the Cattleman's Association meeting next week. Sorry we had to delay, but this situation with Windom's death and now an attempt on Matt's life, has Joe wondering if this is tied into some decision the Association or City Council made that riled someone up."

"I know, he told me and asked if I could think of anything that would cause someone to become violent. I've racked my brain and can't think of anything."

"Me either, but I hope we can figure it out."

He put a ten-dollar bill on the table and left. His truck was parked nearby. He climbed in, rolled down his window, and pulled out his phone. Luckily, he still had the number for the No Limits office in Florida programmed in.

His call was answered on the second ring. "Good morning, No Limits. How may I direct your call?"

"This is Ike Brickman for Ian Grant."

"Let me check and see if he is available, Mr. Brickman."

Ike listened to the music that started when she put him on hold. Just as he wondered if Ian would take the call, it was answered. "Mr. Brickman, hello. I'm surprised to hear from you. I hope Rylee has everything under control there?"

"It's Rylee I'm calling about. She was shot last night trying to save someone's life in one of the local bars."

"Dear God, please tell me she survived and will recover."

"Yes, the doctors have every confidence she will make a full recovery. However, I felt it would be wise to let her family know, but we don't have contact information for her parents, and hoped you could help."

There was a long pause, so long Ike thought the call had been dropped. "Mr. Grant?"

"Yes, I apologize. It's just… well, your statement caught me off guard. I can only assume she didn't tell you why you couldn't call her parents?"

"No, she gave no reason."

"I hate to break confidence, and may regret this, but it seems only fair you know. Rylee's parents are deceased. They died in a boating accident in the Keys two years ago. Rylee has rejected all suggestions regarding grief counseling, but she has not taken their deaths well. In fact, she still speaks of them as if they were alive."

"Dear God, I had no idea, and she has no other family?"

"She has a brother. He's in the Marines, and I believe he'd still out of country. We have him listed as next-of-kin and can probably contact him. Would you like us to try?"

"Very much. If you reach him, have him call me and I can keep him updated on her condition."

"Of course, thank you for calling, Mr. Brickman. Rylee is like family and a valued employee. I want to make sure she has the best of care."

"I'll make sure of that, Mr. Grant. Thank you for your time."

"Let me know if there is anything we can do, Mr. Brickman. Anything at all."

"Thank you. Have a good day."

Ike pocketed his phone and sat there, staring out of the window. Why wouldn't Rylee tell him her parents were dead? He pulled his phone back out and called Matt. "Hey, Dad. What's up?"

"I was on my way to speak with Joe about the shooting and called Rylee's boss. Did you know her parents are dead?"

"Say what? No, she's always texting them and talking about something one of her parents said or did. You must be mistaken."

"No, her boss said they died in a boating accident two years ago, and she took it hard."

"Well, that's understandable, but still odd that she doesn't want people to know."

"Odd is one word for it."

"So, what about her brother? She said he's in the Marines."

"Her boss said he would try to contact her brother, and if he does, will put us in touch."

"Then you've done all you can do."

"All except find out who tried to kill you, and why. I'm headed over to Joe's office and then to the hospital. I have my phone if you need me."

"Thanks, Dad. Everything's under control here. Talk to you later."

Ike once more pocketed his phone, started the truck, and drove over to the police station. Joe was in his office, staring morosely at the monitor of the computer on his desk. "You look like a man who just bit into something rotten." Ike commented as he opened the door and looked in.

"I feel like it," Joe motioned him in. "Close the door."

Ike took a seat and waited for Joe to speak. After a moment, Joe pushed back from the desk and turned his attention to Ike. "More than fifty people in the bar, and not one of them can give a description of the shooter."

"Matt said the man was wearing a full-face covering, like a ski mask."

"That's what everyone says."

"And no one saw him leave or got a look at his vehicle?"

"Not a one."

"They were probably too scared to do more than get the hell out of Dodge," Ike commented.

"Maybe. Did Ms. Monroe see anything?"

"I haven't asked. She *was* shot, you know, and in surgery last night."

"I'm aware. Are you going over there to check on her today?"

"Thought I might."

"Then ask her."

"You can do that just as well as me."

"But she's *your* fiancé."

Ike saw the smirk on Joe's face. "Someone had to check on her, and she doesn't have any family here." Ike didn't think of that statement as a lie. He wasn't going to reveal anything about Rylee's personal life without her permission.

"Still, she's comfortable with you and–"

The ring of Ike's phone interrupted, and Joe fell silent as Ike pulled out the phone. He glanced at the face of the phone before answering. "Rylee?"

"Would you get Matt and go to my condo. Tell Matt to get both the memory cards and my laptop. He'll know what you're talking about. Then have Chief Rogers meet you here at the hospital. There's something he needs to see, and it's important."

"Can you tell me what it is?" The call and the request surprised Ike.

"No, you have to see it. You have to do this or—never mind, I'll call Matt."

"Rylee, I didn't–" Ike didn't get a chance to finish his sentence. She'd already hung up. He looked at Joe. "Give me a minute."

Then he called Matt. "Rylee called and–"

"I've got her on hold."

"Tell her I'll come to the hospital and get her key from her belongings, and meet you there."

"Will do."

Ike pocketed his phone and addressed Joe. "Are you going to be here for a while?"

"That's my plan. What's going on?"

"I don't know, but I'm going to find out. I'll call you in an hour or less if possible."

"And that's all you can tell me?"

"It's all I know," Ike stood. "Be talking to you soon."

It didn't take long to get to the hospital. He was granted access to Rylee's room and found her sitting up, bare legs hanging off the edge of the bed as she struggled to disengage from the IV and monitors.

"What the heck are you doing?"

"I need to get out of here."

"No, you don't. Not until the doctor says you're fit."

"No." She yelped as she snatched the IV from her arm and then started yanking the monitor patches loose.

"Rylee, stop." Ike quickly moved over to her and tried to take her hands to stop her.

"Don't!" She slapped at him. "You don't understand? We found something. Something that might help find the person who killed Donny Caldwell and Mark Windom." She slid off the bed, gave a little squeak, and then made a grab for him as her legs gave way beneath her.

Ike scooped her up in his arms and placed her back on the bed. "Matt's going to meet me at your condo, just like you asked. I just need the key. Do you have it?"

"It's in my belongings." She pointed to a bag on the table beside the bed.

Just then, a nurse ran in. "What in the world is going on in here."

"A tantrum," Ike said, and moved aside for the nurse.

"Let's get you hooked back up. Sir, maybe you should leave for now."

"I agree," Ike cut a glance at Rylee. "I'll be back."

"With the—you know," she gave the nurse the side-eye.

"Yes, just don't do anything else foolish, okay?"

"Fine, just hurry."

Ike didn't bother replying, he just grabbed her keyring from the plastic bag on the table and left. It dawned on him as he exited the hospital that he wasn't sure which condo she owned, so he called Matt. "What's Rylee's address?"

"She's in 402."

"Okay, I'll be waiting there for you."

"On my way."

Ike had no trouble finding Rylee's condo. When he unlocked the door and stepped inside, he stopped and looked around. This place looked nothing like Rylee, at least the woman he'd started to know. This must have been one of the rental units Sharon owned. He remembered the talk about Rylee's company leasing, and then later wanting to purchase a place.

Sharon probably made out like a bandit. Ike smiled. Sharon normally did. She was a smart businesswoman. He went into the living area, noticing the open floor plan, and saw the laptop sitting on the table. Ike started to open it, but refrained. It was probably passworded.

He took a seat at the table to wait, and as he did, he thought about Rylee. He still couldn't figure out why she was loath to let anyone know her parents were dead. God knew he'd suffer unspeakable grief when he lost his parents, but he didn't think that would prompt him to pretend they were still alive. There had to be more to the tale than Ian had revealed.

His thoughts then turned to what had gotten her shot. Did she care so much for Matt that she'd risk her own life, or was the act something she would do for a friend she was just getting to know? Either way, it was brave, and he'd never forget she saved his son.

That led him to think about Matt. Why wasn't Matt keen on dating Rylee? Or was he? After all, they were at a honky tonk, dancing when she was shot. Is that something you did with someone who was just a friend?

His phone rang, and he pulled it from his pocket. The caller ID read *Unknown,* and he almost dismissed the call, but thinking it could be the hospital, answered. "Hello?"

"Is this Ike Brickman?" a deep male voice asked.

"Who's asking?"

"Chief Rayce Monroe. Ian Grant gave me this number and said I should call and speak with Ike Brickman about my sister, Rylee."

"Yes, Chief Monroe, thank you for calling. Rylee was shot and is in the hospital, but is recovering, and the doctors say they don't expect any complications."

"Thank God, what happened that she was shot?"

"She was with my son, Matthew, at one of the local honky tonks, and someone wearing a ski mask shot her." Ike knew that wasn't exactly what happened, but it was close enough. "No one knows why."

"Was the guy caught?"

"Not yet, but the police are doing everything they can to identify him."

"Should I try to get leave to come there?"

"She's in no danger. When she leaves the hospital, she's welcome to stay at my family's ranch where she'll be safe."

"I appreciate that, sir. Could you or someone there please keep me updated?"

"Absolutely."

"Thank you, sir. Should I wait to call Rylee?"

"Why don't you give her a day?"

"Of course. Again, thank you. I appreciate you looking out for her."

"Don't worry, we'll take care of her."

"Thank you, sir."

"You bet."

Just then, Matt walked into the condo. "Where are these memory cards Rylee mentioned?" Ike asked.

Matt pulled one from his pocket as he walked over to the table and then pointed at the side of the laptop where a card protruded from of the reader slot. "Is she okay?"

"She's fine, son. Just fit to be tied to get his laptop and those cards. You want to tell me what's so all-fired important about them?"

"I think it'd be best if you wait and see for yourself."

"Fine, then grab the laptop and let's go. I'll call and have the Chief meet us there."

"Okay," Matt picked up the laptop and headed back out, as Ike placed the call.

On the drive over, Ike wondered what could be so important on those memory cards, and how he was going to tell Rylee he'd spoken to her brother and knew about her parents.

He grunted in frustration. It seemed like ever since Donny Caldwell's death, his own life had gotten a lot more complicated.

Ike hated complicated.

Chapter Sixteen

It took longer than expected to get in to see Rylee. When the nurses at the station saw three men headed down the hallway, one of them ran interference. "Pardon me. Sirs? Sirs?"

Ike, who led the way, stopped. "I'm Ike Brickman, on the list of approved visitors for Rylee Monroe. This is my son, also on the list, and Chief Joe Rogers."

"Police business, ma'am," Joe added.

"Oh, well, well I guess it will be fine."

"Thank you," Ike touched his finger to his hat, then continued down the hall. To his surprise, when he tapped on the door, it was his mother's voice who answered.

"Come on in."

"Mom?" Ike stepped inside and glanced around. Rylee was sitting at the small table in front of the window with his parents. And from the looks of things, playing Rummy. "What are you and Dad doing here?"

"Visiting a friend," Asa replied. "Your eyes failing you, son?" He glanced at Matt and the Chief as they entered. "What's going on?"

"We brought your laptop and the memory cards," Matt said as he carried the laptop to Rylee.

"Right here," she patted the table.

Matt set the laptop on the table as she rose, then gave her a hug. "You doing okay?"

"Yes, I'm fine. Sore, but fine. They don't keep you in the bed long, which is wonderful. It's so good to see you."

"Thank you," he took her hand.

"What are friends for?"

"Don't make light of it. I owe you."

"Then when they cut me loose, you can take me dancing again. And more drone lessons."

"You got it."

"Ms. Monroe?" Chief Rogers spoke up.

"Yes, sir?"

"Ike says you have something to show me?"

"I do. Can Mrs. Georgia and Mr. Asa stay?"

Everyone looked at Joe and, after a moment, he shrugged. "I reckon that'll be okay."

"Great." She opened the laptop and, after a few moments, turned the computer around so everyone could see the screen. "This is the footage captured by one of the cameras in town. As you'll see, it shows the hit and run."

She played the footage, noticing how Georgia glanced away when Donny was hit by the truck. As soon as the truck turned the corner and disappeared, she stopped the playback.

"I can't tell anything about the driver," Chief Rogers said.

"No, the camera was too far away. But No Limits authorized me to purchase software to enhance the video." She turned the laptop around, typed on the keyboard and then turned it again so everyone could see. "And once enhanced, this is what we see."

This time, everyone could see a man's profile as the truck turned the corner. He had a full beard, and wore a ball cap pulled down low, shadowing his eyes.

"Anyone recognize this man?" Joe asked.

Everyone in the room looked around at one another, either answered "no" or shook their heads.

"There's one other thing you need to make note of," Rylee added and backed up the playback a couple of seconds. "See right here," she pointed to the back windshield, just past the driver's left shoulder. "See that? It's either a sticker or some emblem painted on the window. Have you seen that before?"

"It looks familiar, but I can't place it," Joe replied.

"Okay, well, you also need to see this." As she talked, she switched out the memory cards. "Mr. Asa, you might remember this. You and Matt were filming the day Brent Corsa died in the car accident and when Matt scanned through the cards, he found this."

She played the footage of Brent's car and the truck appearing behind him, bearing down on the car. When the back of the truck was in full view, she paused the playback. "First, take note that there's no tag. Second, look here," she pointed to the window. "The same sticker."

Joe walked over to get a closer look. "I'll be damned. Can I take the memory cards, and get a copy of your enhancement?"

"Of course," she removed the memory card Matt had given her and handed it, along with her own, to the Chief. "And in case you need validation, the mayor was with me when we first viewed the footage from the traffic camera, and made this copy."

"Well, I have to say you've provided me more than we've been able to come up with. Thank you, young lady."

"I hope it helps."

"So do I." He looked at the other people. "You good folks have a nice day. Ike, I'll be talking to you."

"Yep. Be safe, Joe."

Once Joe left, Ike turned his attention to Rylee. "Should you be out of the bed?"

"I should," she replied with a smile. "Thanks to your parents, the doctor is going to release me today."

"Into our custody, so to speak," Georgia added. "She heard from her boss to take two weeks to heal and work from home, so we're taking her to the ranch. She can work from there."

Ike looked at Rylee. "Is that what you want?"

"Are you kidding? I'll go nuts if I stay here. I'm in their debt."

"No, honey, we're in yours," Georgia said. "You saved Matt and we can't ever repay that."

"You don't have to," Rylee said and reached for Georgia's hand. "He's my friend, and I only did what anyone would have done."

"I don't know that to be a fact, but it speaks to your goodness that you believe it," Georgia said and released her hand. "Now, Asa and I are going to go get things set up. Is there anything you need from your condo?"

"Yes, but I was hoping I could go gather my things myself. Or at least with someone?"

"I'll take you," Ike volunteered.

"Are you sure you don't mind?"

"Not at all."

"Good, then I'll go help Pop and Gigi get things set up." Matt said. "How about we put her in the downstairs guestroom? That way, she doesn't have to climb stairs, and it's close to the back porch. On nice days she can sit there and work."

"Sounds good," Ike agreed.

"Then let's get to it," Matt said and looked at his grandparents.

They both stood, and Asa spoke around a smile. "Yeah, I reckon Ike needs to have a moment or two alone with his fiancé."

Ike shot his mother a look as she chuckled, and she glanced away. "I'll deliver the patient as soon as she's discharged, and we gather her things."

"Then we'll see you later," Asa replied, and they all left.

It seemed like a deep well of silence when it was only him and Rylee. She closed her laptop and carried it over to the bed where her plastic bag of belongings lay. "I didn't tell them that. The doctor did."

"It doesn't matter."

"Then why does your face look like a thundercloud?"

Ike had stewed on it all night and wished he knew a diplomatic way to broach the subject, but since he didn't, he approached it the only way he knew. "I thought we had some measure of trust between us."

"We do," she replied.

"Do we?"

"Yes. Why would you even say that?"

"Because you lied to me."

"I did not."

He walked over to stand in front of her, all too aware that the height difference gave him a dominance in the situation. "Then let's call it being deliberately misleading."

"What does that mean?"

Ike wouldn't beat around the bush anymore. "Why can't I call your parents?"

She turned away and started fiddling with the items in the bag. "I told you, I don't–"

"Want to be honest and tell me they're dead?"

Her head jerked around so fast in his direction, it should have given her whiplash. "Who told you that?"

"It doesn't matter. It's true, isn't it?"

She shook her head and backed away, and it hit him. She seemed genuinely afraid or traumatized, and he almost regretted opening this dialogue. But something told him this wound had been festering long enough, and it was time to lance that boil and let the poison out.

"Rylee, look at me,"

"I don't want to," her head lowered, and she stared at the bed.

"Rylee, look at me and tell me the truth. Your parents are dead."

She shook her head again, refusing to look at him. Ike tried twice more and each time she refused to speak or even look his way. His patience hit a wall, and he reacted stronger than he intended. He grabbed her arm and jerked her around to face him. "Tell me. What happened to your parents?"

He thought she would refuse to speak and was shocked when she jerked away and hissed at him. "It's my fault. They're dead because of me. Are you happy now Ike?"

Happy was the last word he'd used to describe how he felt at that moment. Confused was at the top of the list. "That's not true. Your boss told me. They died in a boating accident in the Keys two years ago."

"On a boat I chartered to get away for a few days, try my hand at fishing and just basically decompress. Only I was wrapped up in a project, so I told them to go and not let the trip be wasted and they did. They went, and they died and it's my fault."

"You can't believe that."

"Don't you get it? I chartered that boat, which means it was supposed to be me on it when it sank in that storm. But..." Her voice cracked, and she put her hands over her face. "I killed them, Ike. I killed my parents."

Ike had never in his life understood until that moment, but finally knew what it meant when people said something broke their heart. Seeing her so broken and grief-stricken broke his heart for her.

Considering nothing other than offering comfort, he pulled her into his arms. "Shhh," he whispered against her hair as she buried her face against his chest and cried. "It's okay. I've got you. I've got you."

Ike didn't know how long they stood there. It took a long time for her to stop crying and when she finally looked up at him, there was such a look of misery in her eyes, it made him blink back sudden moisture. "I miss them so much."

"I know you do. But you have to stop blaming yourself. You're a smart woman and you know it wasn't your fault, but I guess it was easier to stay mad at yourself and try to pretend it wasn't real, rather than let all that loss and grief take you."

She nodded. "They're gone and Rayce is never home and– God, listen to me whine. How pathetic."

"No, you're not. And finish what you were going to say."

She looked down. "I feel alone. There's just me and no one to–to tether me. I feel cut adrift, and I don't belong anymore."

"Yes, you do," he argued and took her hand. "You have me and Matt, my folks and Sharon. You're not alone."

"Thank you, but you're just being kind and you don't have to."

"One thing people don't accuse me of is excess kindness," he argued. "So, when I say you have us, I mean it. Matt already sees you as a friend, and my folks would never have invited you to the ranch if they didn't care about you."

"And you?" she asked in what he perceived as a timid tone.

This wasn't a time for lies, but he felt tempted. Ike had tried to avoid processing the feelings he had for Rylee, and he didn't feel very comfortable about the way it was all pressing in on him now, but he wouldn't lie to her.

"I like you."

"Like a friend?"

"Maybe. Maybe more. I don't know, Rylee. It's been a thousand years since I was interested in a woman and I'm rusty. Off balance. And the age thing bothers me."

"I understand. I've never been in love, so I don't know what it feels like, but I do like you, Ike. Maybe more. I don't know, but I do know I want to get to know you. If you'll let me."

"I think that's a fine idea."

She finally smiled, and color him as waxing poetic, but it felt like the sun had just emerged from behind a cloud. He wasn't ready to admit he wanted more from her than friendship. When he said the age difference was an issue, he meant it.

And unfortunately for himself and her, Ike had a hard time changing his mind about things. It might have been better if she'd taken an interest in one of his sons, because a year from now Ike might feel the same way.

He'd want her, think about the *what ifs,* and never make a move for fear of becoming something he despised. An old man with a trophy girlfriend who would surely become disenchanted with him when she started to see things clearly.

And if there was one experience he didn't want in life, it was to have his heart broken. He'd escaped that so far, and that's how he wanted it to stay.

Chapter Seventeen

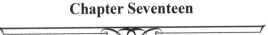

Ike heard laughter coming from the kitchen as he descended the stairs. It was a sound he hadn't heard in the house for a long time. Until now. Over the last week, he'd heard it often. Whenever Matt or Tom, his parents or even his daughter Liz came over and started talking with Rylee, it wasn't long before people were laughing.

She had that effect on people with the million questions she had about the ranch, the way things work, the land and history, and a host of other topics. Her eyes perceived what folks who'd spent their lives there had grown blind to. The color of the sky and clouds, the way the animals sniffed the air, and how nervous they became at the onset of a storm.

Rylee was curious about everything and found delight in nearly everything. Ike liked that about her. He entered the kitchen to find Rylee standing beside Bear at the stove. Bear grew up on the ranch. His father and mother had spent most of their lives there and lived in one of the larger cabins on the ranch. Bear's mother, Elsie, was the housekeeper at the ranch, and his father, Claude, was one of the best horse trainers in the state, who also trained tracking animals and oversaw the wranglers.

Bear joined the Marines after graduating high school, served for a decade, and came home missing a leg. Ike offered to hire him, and Bear said he loved to cook. To everyone's shock, he was good at it, and since then, he'd been the ranch's official chef.

His wife, Ann, and their two kids, Benny and Cathy, lived in another of the cabins on the ranch. Ann taught at the elementary school where their kids attended.

At the moment, Bear was overseeing Rylee as she flipped a pancake, while Matt, Tom and Liz sat at the bar, drinking coffee, and talking.

"Good morning," Ike said as he entered the room.

"Morning, Daddy," Liz said, and got up to pour him a cup of coffee.

"Morning Dad," Matt and Tom echoed.

"Good morning," Ike echoed the greeting and added "thanks, honey," to Liz as she handed him the cup of steaming coffee.

"Good morning," Bear said over his shoulder.

"Morning, Bear. How are Ann and the kids?"

"Fine and dandy, thanks, sir."

"And you?" Ike stepped over to lean on the counter beside the stove where Rylee stood.

"I'm just peachy, thank you. Bear, let me do the pancakes."

"Did you hold a gun on him?"

Everyone laughed, and Ike added. "Bear doesn't let anyone touch his pots and pans."

"Well, I'm not just anyone," she said with a little sass in her tone, and then lowered her voice. "I'm the woman who just gave him the recipe for the world's best pancakes. My mother's recipe. I had it on my computer and gave it to him."

"World's best?" Ike glanced at Bear.

Bear nodded. "Wait 'till you taste them."

"Well, in that case, I'll definitely have to try them out."

"Just be forewarned," Rylee put a golden-brown pancake on the towering stack and slathered butter on it. "Once you taste these pancakes, you're going to be my slave forever."

"Slave, huh?"

"Forever," she nodded and grinned. "It's good to see you smile."

"And you," he said.

"It's ready," Bear announced. "You want to eat in the dining room?"

"Let's eat here in the kitchen," Liz suggested.

"Works for me." Matt was the first to agree.

"Then grab a plate and dig in," Ike said.

Within minutes, everyone was seated at the table, digging into a meal of pancakes, eggs, steak, and bacon.

Ike sampled the pancakes and glanced at Rylee in surprise. "This is a good pancake."

"Feel the need to be my slave yet?"

"Not yet."

"Then keep eating."

He smiled and turned his attention to his breakfast as conversation flowed around him. It occurred to him that his children had accepted Rylee as one of their own. Even Liz, and she wasn't the easiest to get along with.

"Tom said you have people coming in today to look at some of your horses?" Rylee directed her inquiry to Ike.

"We have a few horses we might sell. Their earnings aren't what we want, but they'll make good breeding stock for someone. And we're negotiating stud fees for a few of the stallions."

"I know nothing about that sort of thing. Can you tell me about your horses?"

Ike glanced over at Tom. "You want to handle that question?"

"Sure," Tom wiped his mouth and took a drink of orange juice. "First, what no one has told you, Dad is one of the top performance horse trainers in the world. So, is Bear's father."

"And so are you," Ike added. "Matt as well, when we can get him interested."

"What does that mean?" Rylee asked. "A performance horse trainer?"

"Basically, it's someone who trains horse for showing or racing, riding, working with cows or even police work." Tom answered. "In our case, we train reined cow horses."

"And that is?" Rylee asked.

"Horses that can perform specific maneuvers, like circling the cow, turning it in a specified manner and performing a reining pattern."

"What's that?"

"It's a precise pattern of spins, circles and stops."

"And you train your horses to do that because?"

"They earn us money," Ike said. "The horses we're showing today for sale aren't our top earners, but they come from excellent stock and in time could be real money-makers. We have earners in the National Reining Horse Association, National Reined Cow Horse Association, and point-earners through the American Quarter Horse Association."

"I'm guessing that's impressive?"

Ike chuckled. "Yeah, it's impressive."

"Can I watch?" Rylee's smile abruptly faded. "I'm sorry, I am butting in?"

"Not at all," Ike said, and reached over to pat her arm. "You're welcome to watch."

"Thank you," she beamed at him. "You know, Tom and Matt promised to take me riding on Saturday, and I talked Liz into joining. Want to come with us?"

"I can take the chuck wagon out to the river and set up," Bear offered. "Set up the tents and make a weekend of it."

Ike almost said no, but the hopeful expression on Rylee's face changed his mind. "Why not? Bear, bring the family, all of them, your wife, kids, and parents. I'll tell Pop and mom to join."

"Yay," Rylee's smile was so bright and excited, it warmed Ike. It'd been a long time since anyone was excited about camping, and that was something he'd always loved.

"But for now, we need to get moving," Ike said. "Tom, I'll meet you at the barn in half an hour. I'm going to ride over and check on the folks."

"Sounds good," Tom looked at Matt. "You're still helping today, right?"

"Are you kidding? I'm gonna kick your butt in the slide."

"I got a hundred that says different," Tom argued good-naturedly.

"What is a slide?" Rylee asked.

"Bringing your horse to a sliding stop," Liz finally joined in.

"Can you do that?"

Liz shook her head. "I'm the numbers girl."

"But you ride horses, right?"

Tom grinned. "Junior dressage champion three years running. She rides like a rich white girl."

Everyone laughed at that, and Liz threw her napkin at Tom. "Brat."

"Princess."

Liz looked at Rylee. "Are you still game on setting up that security for the ranch's server?"

"You bet."

"Great, let's go to the office and get started. How long do you think it will take?"

"A while, but I can use something I've already developed and adapt it, which will shorten the development time."

"What's all that?" Ike asked.

"She's going to shore up our security," Liz replied. "Like she did for the drones."

"You put in security for the drones?"

"Matt and Mr. Asa work for many businesses and government departments. They need to make sure their data can't be hacked, so I wrote the software and we're currently testing and tweaking."

"And how much are we paying for that?" Ike directed the question to Matt.

"Nothing."

"Nothing?" Ike glanced again at Rylee.

"Friends help friends," she replied.

"That's a lot of help."

"No, it's not. It's something that's easy for me, and you all have been so gracious to me it's the least I can do. Besides, I enjoy helping people I care about."

"Well, we should pay."

"I'd call room and board on this magnificent ranch damn good pay," Rylee argued. "You've all been so kind, looking out for me and teaching me to ride, and-" she glanced over her shoulder at Bear. "Letting me invade your kitchen."

Then she looked at Ike. "I want to do it. Okay?"

He nodded and stood. "Then you girls get to it, and you boys get with it too."

"Yes, sir," Matt replied and got to his feet. "Thanks, Bear. It was good."

"Glad to hear that. Have a good day."

"You too."

As he headed out of the room, Tom got up and followed. Liz called out, "Tom, where are those invoices for last month?"

"In the barn office. Want me to get them for you?"

"I'll walk with you. Rylee? Meet me in the office?"

"Sure."

Rylee stood and started clearing the table, but Bear nudged her out of the way. "Go get to it, shorty. I got this."

"Shorty?" She put one hand on a hip and jutted her chin up to look at Bear, who stood a full foot taller and a hundred pounds heavier.

"Shorty."

She smiled. "Okay, thanks. Can you teach me some more about cooking later?"

"Sure, you can help with dinner."

"Thank you," she stood on tiptoe to kiss his cheek, then turned toward Ike. "Do you mind if I walk out with you? I want to see the sky before we get to work."

"That'd be fine."

They went outside, and when they reached the bottom of the steps, Rylee stopped and looked out over the land. "I've never seen anything this beautiful in my life. Thank you for letting me stay here. I feel... never mind. Just thank you."

Ike felt like she was afraid to say what she felt, and that bothered him. "No, finish that. You feel what?"

She stared up at the sky and then at him. "Like I'm not alone. It's nice, and I appreciate you letting me feel like part of a family for a little while. I promise I'll try not to overstay my welcome."

"I don't believe you could."

The words were out before he could rein them in, and from her expression, she was as surprised as he. "Careful, Mr. Brickman," she said as she looked directly into his eyes. "A girl could get her hopes up hearing something like that."

Ike didn't know what to say, so he acted instead, leaned down and kissed her cheek. "Go do your thing, Rylee Monroe, and meet us at the barn at ten."

"I'll be there." She said, smiled and turned away.

Ike watched her head down the drive toward the office, then climbed into his truck. It bothered him how much he enjoyed Rylee being here. Even though the kiss on the cheek he'd just given her was the only physical contact they'd had since that night at the bar, he felt like they were forming a kind of connection.

And that might be more dangerous than lust.

Chapter Eighteen

"Done," Rylee announced, saved the program, and glanced at Liz. "Are you in a coma yet?"

"Actually, it's pretty interesting," Liz responded. "I took a few programming classes in college and liked it, but Dad needed me to learn about finance, how to invest, how to get the best return on the money, how to keep track of everything, protect it, and how to keep the wolves at bay so he could focus on running things."

Rylee studied the beautiful blonde woman sitting beside her. She looked more like a movie star than a number cruncher. Rylee knew within an hour of their initial meeting that Liz was smart, intuitive, and distrustful of people she didn't know.

That didn't offend Rylee at all. She simply accepted that's who Liz was, and somehow that seemed to make it easier. She and Liz became friends before the evening ended, and now Liz came by almost every day to visit.

Rylee deliberated for a moment before responding. "Want me to teach you?"

She noticed the way Liz's eyes widened a bit, then the way the corners of her mouth turned up until a full-blown smile took control of her face. "Oh yes, I do."

"Great. Let's pick a day—probably evening, since I have to get back to the office soon. Meet me at the condo. I'll order takeout and after we eat, we'll dive in."

"Super," Liz smiled. "But I'll supply the food, and I'm not opposed to paying."

"No, I wouldn't ever do this for money."

"Then why do it at all?"

Rylee didn't have to think about her answer. "Because I believe you're honest, have integrity, and won't use what I teach you to hurt anyone."

"What makes you so sure?"

Rylee smiled. "Because I know things."

That prompted a laugh from Liz. "Yeah, I bet you do. Say, can I ask a personal question?"

"You can ask."

Liz rolled her eyes. "You sound like my Dad."

"That's a compliment, right?"

"Depends. So, here's my question. What's going on with you and Dad?"

"Is there something going on?" Rylee wasn't comfortable talking about her and Ike. She knew what she wanted from him, at least for the moment, but couldn't speak for him.

"Oh yeah, something's going on. Do you know who the last houseguest we had was?"

"Obviously not."

"One of the billionaire cowboy wannabes who showed up here when I was fifteen, basically wanting Dad to teach him how to do what we do. Dad let him spend the night, but sent him on his way the next day when the guy slept until nine."

"Why would that make him send the man away?"

"Because if you sleep until nine, you're never going to learn to do what we do. Everyone here is up before the sun."

"Oh, well then, I feel honored I haven't been shown the door. Yet."

"And that brings us to the topic at hand," Liz said, and turned her head to glance out of the window where the barns and one of the paddocks were visible. "He likes you being here."

"How do you know?"

Liz turned her gaze to Rylee. "He's smiled and laughed more since you've been here than he has in the last decade."

Rylee didn't know how to comment on that statement, so she remained silent. "You like him, don't you?" Liz asked.

"Yes."

"Why?"

"Well," Rylee paused, unsure how to answer. "He seems like an honorable man, perhaps a bit hot-tempered, and not entirely patient, but someone who honestly cares about the land and the lives on it, human and animal. He's…" She stopped because she almost revealed her attraction to Ike."

"He's what?" Liz prompted, and when Rylee didn't answer, added. "If you'll trust me to teach me to do what you do, then trust me on this."

"I don't know if I can."

"Why?"

"Because he's your Dad."

"Yes, he is, and I want to know how you feel about him."

"I feel–I feel like I want to get to know him. When we went out that night, I saw a side of him that... I'm sorry. I don't do this well."

"Do what?"

"Share. I don't share well—how I feel. Ask me anything that requires analytical thinking, and I'll chatter for hours, but–but I'm not good at telling people how I feel."

"I understand," Liz nodded and stood. "How would Thursday work for you?"

"Thursday?"

"To teach me."

"You still want to do that?"

Liz laughed. "Rylee, it's fine that you're not ready to trust me with your feelings. I'm not sure I'm ready to trust you with mine. But I like you, and I trust you not to hurt my Dad. So yes, I surely want to move forward with the lessons."

"Terrific." Rylee felt a sense of relief. "Then Thursdays, I can be home by six."

"It's a date," Liz turned toward the door, then stopped. "The first Thursday you're home."

Rylee smiled at her. "Yes, it's a date."

"Okay, I'm going to work. If you need me, I'll be right here."

"Okay, thanks." Rylee headed for the door and just as she stepped outside her phone rang.

"Ian, hello. This is a surprise."

"I trust you're on the mend?"

"I am. Honestly, I can go back to the office now."

"Perhaps, but your doctor said two weeks, so two it is. And I'm told you are running things efficiently via remote."

She chuckled. "I'm probably driving them insane."

"You're doing your job. Now, the reason for my call is to let you know, I've requested the Police Chief have the keys to Brent's house delivered to you. You can take as long as you need, but when you've finished going through it, please let me know. We need to hire someone to pack everything and have it shipped to the family."

"Absolutely, and thank you."

"I don't know how it could, but if it provides even a minute clue to who is responsible for the terrible mystery of those murders, I'm eager to help."

"I appreciate it and will be as fast as possible."

"Excellent. Call if you have need of me."

"I will, thank you, sir."

"Take care and don't overdo."

"No sir, I won't."

"We'll talk soon."

"Yes, sir. Have a good day."

She started toward the barn, but a thought had her stopping and pulling out her phone again. Chief Rogers had given her his cell phone number, and they'd spoken several times about the footage she turned over to him. This time, her call was about something different, and she hoped he would be receptive.

"Good morning Ms. Monroe, what can I do for you?"

"Hello, Chief Rogers. I apologize for bothering you, but I have an idea I want to run by you and see what you think."

"I'm listening."

"Thank you. First, were there any cell phones recovered from Brent Corsa's car?"

"Yes, two. Both were damaged."

"Did you try to retrieve whatever was on those phones or request the records from the carrier?"

"No, why?"

"Because if Brent made a copy and then erased that footage, there's a chance he communicated with whoever he made the copy for, and if we can get that number, maybe we can figure who is behind the deaths of Donnie Caldwell and Mark Windom, and the attempt on Matt Brickman."

"Something we considered, but our techs couldn't do anything with the phones, and without cause we can't request the records."

"How about letting me and my hardware guys make a stab at it?"

There was a momentary pause before the Chief responded. "I don't see why not. Want me to drop them by your office?"

"Yes, please. I'll let the staff know and thank you."

"Thanks for your help, talk soon."

"Yes, sir. Bye."

Pleased that he'd agreed, Rylee pocketed her phone. The walk to the barn was about half a mile and quite pleasant. She thought, not for the first time since she'd been there, that she'd love to have this kind of place where you could wander for days and never leave your own land.

As she drew near the barn, she saw men gathered at the paddock fence, watching riders in the paddock. Rylee walked over and stood off to one side. Within moments, she was moving closer to the fence.

It was like something from a movie. Tom and Matt were on horseback and what magnificent horses they rode. She stood there, mesmerized, as she watched them race their horses from one side of the paddock to the other. As they drew near the fence, the horses suddenly did an odd maneuver where they looked like they were going to sit on their rears, but simply skidded to a stop.

She'd never seen anything like that. Matt and Tom roped cows, herded half a dozen across the paddock, and even spun their horses around in a tight circle like a ballet dancer. It was impressive, and darn, if it didn't look a little sexy as well, the way the horse and rider acted as one.

It wasn't hard to figure out that it impressed the men watching. There was a lot of chatter for a minute, and then everything went silent. Matt and Tom glanced toward the gate, and after a second, everyone else did.

Rylee felt like a star-struck teenage girl when she saw Ike ride into the arena. She'd never been a woman who harbored a secret crush on cowboys. That changed in the space of a heartbeat.

Matt rode over to where she stood at the fence, dismounted, and looped his arm over the top rail. "That's Dad's baby. Well, newest baby. Hot Smoke."

"I can see the Smoke part," she remarked. The horse was the color of smoke, a deep gray that had a lighter sheen when the sunlight hit it at a certain angle. His mane and tail were ebony, long, thick, and shiny. If an animal could be described as sexy, this was the horse that fit the label.

"Why Hot?" she asked, trying not to pay attention to the man on the horse.

"Dad thinks he might pass Silver Smoke, his stud, in earnings."

Rylee knew nothing about the horse business, so didn't understand the statement.

"How do horses earn money?"

"These are performance horses, so exactly like the term implies, we enter them into shows for cash prizes and to increase the rate of their stud fees. Hot's sire, Silver Smoke has lifetime earnings exceeding twenty-five million, commands a ten-thousand-dollar stud fee and is booked for the next four years."

"Twenty-five million?" That stunned her. "And Hot? Has he earned anything?"

"So far, about three million. We'll get thirty-eight hundred as his stud fee this year, and haven't started booking for next year because we expect his earnings to increase. He was a finalist at the 2020 NRCHA Snaffle Bit Futurity and the National Stock Horse Association Snaffle Bit futurity."

"I had no idea," she murmured, watching as Ike directed his horse through a performance that amazed her. She knew Matt was talking, but she couldn't focus. Her attention was on Ike.

"Hey, earth to Rylee," Matt's tap on her arm snapped her attention back to him.

"Sorry, I was–"

"Yeah, I know."

She felt her face grow hot, but looked at him anyway. "Sorry. I've never seen anything like this and your dad–well, he–never mind."

"I get it. He's a master at what he does."

"Obviously." She agreed.

"Did he tell you he's a bonafied horse whisperer?"

"Is that a real thing?"

"Oh yeah, Pop is too. Seems like it's a thing in our family."

"Are you?"

He shrugged. "I get by, but Dad is the real deal. I think Tom is too."

"This is a whole new world." Rylee glanced at the people watching, "And they're all either mesmerized or standing there wishing they could buy that horse and do what your dad does."

"They're standing there trying to figure out if they should even try to buy that horse, or try to get on the stud list."

"Let's say they get on the list. Are there criteria for the mother horse?"

"Oh yeah. Hot's mama is a cutting horse who's won over seventy-five thousand, and is ranked in the top 10 in the 2019 NCHA World Standings in the ten thousand Novice class."

"I'm guessing that's good?"

"Yep." There was a few minutes of silence before Matt spoke again. "So, tell me, my friend. Do you have a crush on my dad?"

Rylee saw his smile and knew that regardless of what she told him, he would still be her friend, so she didn't bother to lie or skirt the truth. "You bet'cha."

"And what're you going to do about it?"

She gnawed her bottom lip for a moment. "I'm not sure yet."

"Want a suggestion?"

"Always."

"Make your move when we're camping."

"Really?"

Matt grinned and climbed back on his horse. "Trust me on this one."

She smiled without comment, but thought about it as he rode away. She had a thing for Ike and wasn't ashamed to admit she'd love to get him into her bed, but she got the idea that when it came to that sort of thing, Ike liked to take the lead.

So, if it meant waiting and hoping that he would, that's what she'd do. And if he never did, that would be proof positive that despite what he might say, he just wasn't interested, or at least not interested enough to stop something like age from getting in the way.

Chapter Nineteen

Ike spotted Riley standing beside the fence and was keenly aware that her attention was on him. He finished talking to one of the buyers, dismounted, and asked a groomer to take care of Hot Smoke.

Her gaze was still on him when he strode over to her. "I've never seen anything like that," she commented. "How do you teach a horse to do that?"

He leaned down and whispered, "It's a secret," then straightened and smiled.

"Matt told me you're a horse whisperer. That all the men in the family are."

Ike wasn't sure how to comment, so he remained silent. No one in his family talked about their ability with animals. It was simply a skill or instinct they'd been born with, and they used it for the benefit of the ranch.

"Does that mean the animals understand you?"

"Yes, I think it does."

"And do you understand them?"

"Every horse trainer understands their animals to some degree. Their sounds, eyes, movements—it all paints a picture of how an animal feels."

"But being a whisperer means a deeper understanding, doesn't it? A connection of some sort?"

"Another surprise from Rylee Monroe."

"I'm a greenhorn, not a dumb bunny. Animals communicate far more than people realize. Just go to a zoo. Some animals will break your heart. Once, I went with my family to Disney. They have this enormous aquarium, and you can walk through halls with towering walls of glass.

"As soon as I stepped inside, I was hit with an almost physical power by a wave of something—something I didn't understand. As soon as I got close to the glass, one dolphin swam over to me. I looked into her eyes–"

"Her?"

"Yes, when our gazes connected, I knew she was female. Just like I knew she was so terribly sad. She was a prisoner and wanted only to be released. It hit me so hard and with such an emotional wallop that I burst into tears. My parents thought someone had said or done something and tried to get me to tell them what was wrong, but I couldn't speak. All I could do was stand there with my hand on that glass, the dolphin's snout on the other side, and our gazes locked. It hurt so bad that I felt like I was physically injured. My parents led me away, and I spent the rest of the day crying. I'll never forget her, and I'll never stop hating that I couldn't give her what she so desperately wanted."

She paused and swiped at the tears that flowed down her face, and Ike marveled at her capacity for compassion. "Then I suppose you understand something about being an animal whisperer, don't you?"

"I don't know. If it meant feeling that kind of pain and desperation, I don't know if I'd want to be."

"I don't blame you, but working with horses hasn't brought me any such experiences, so I'm going to go out on a limb and say what you experienced is an extreme moment that doesn't happen often."

"You're kind for not making fun of me. How do you know that even really happened?"

"Your eyes don't lie."

"I think that's one of the nicest things anyone has ever said to me. Thank you." She swiped at her eyes again and smiled. "I didn't know horses like the ones you breed, and train were such money makers."

Ike recognized she sought to change the conversation to something less emotional and something not about herself, and wondered if she felt uncomfortable about revealing something about her past.

"Well, you either raise cattle or breed horses. I prefer horses."

"But you have cattle, don't you?"

"Yep, Pop has a fondness, so we keep a small herd."

"Define small."

"Couple hundred head. Tom and Pop are talking about ramping up their bull breeding operation. There's money to be made there."

"Is money what's important?" She held her arms out to her sides. "With all this, surely money isn't the primary motivation."

He considered it for a moment, then answered from the heart. "The land, the family and animals who live on it is what matters, but keeping it all healthy and maintained is expensive, so we have to be profitable, or the people and animals suffer, and I can't have that."

Rylee smiled. "Good answer."

"I wasn't aware I was being tested."

"We're all being tested," she replied and looked around. "Every day."

"Something bothering you?" He asked when she gazed out over the land with an expression he read as troubled.

"No more than normal."

"Rylee, don't let Joe or Sharon make you feel you owe the town some debt. We'd all like to find out who's responsible for the killings, but we don't expect you to uncover the guilty party. It's clear to everyone that you're going way beyond the call of duty on this thing, but if you have no answers, that's the end of it. Leave it to the police to do their jobs and find the killer."

"Thank you, but–"

"No buts. You're supposed to be recuperating, and all you've done since you've been here is work. First for Matt and then Liz. You don't have to do that."

"I wanted to."

"Then let us pay."

"No, absolutely not. It's a gift."

"Then let us give you a gift in return."

"You already have. You're letting me stay here and experience all this."

"That's because you need someone to look after you, like the doctor said. Just to make sure there are no setbacks. It's not payment. And there has to be something you want."

"No, there isn't."

"Nothing?"

He noticed the way she gnawed her bottom lip, and her eyes narrowed. "Well?" he verbally nudged. "There is something, isn't there?"

"Yes, but—but you already said yes."

"I did?"

"Yes, you said we could all go camping."

"That's really what you want?"

"Yes."

"Then that's what we'll do. Let me finish here and I'll get the wranglers busy getting the wagons ready." He looked around, spotted Matt, and waved him over. "When you're done here, call Pop and Mom and tell them we're packing up to head for the river. We'll be done here in an hour, so if we get cracking, we can be there and set up before two."

"Sounds good," Matt replied and grinned at Rylee. "You riding a horse or a wagon, city girl."

"A horse please."

"You got it." He turned and rode back to the buyers gathered now at the entrance of the barn.

Rylee smiled at Ike. "This is really nice of you."

"It's the least I can do for the woman who saved my son's life."

"I don't want payment for–"

Ike realized his mistake and interrupted. "It's the least I can do for a friend."

Her smile lit something inside him, but not near as much as her touch when she placed her hand on his arm. "I like you, Ike Brickman. You're a kind man."

"Kind isn't a word most people use to describe me."

"Then they don't see what I do. Oh, look, that man is waving at you. I'm going to go tell Bear I want to help with the cooking."

"Tell him we'll be leaving soon, so get a move on."

"I will." She turned as if to leave, then suddenly pivoted, stepped over and stood on tiptoe to give him a kiss on the cheek. "And I know you're kind, Ike. You have a good heart."

"Thank you, Rylee," he got a charge out of her words and the kiss. Funny how a woman he'd known for a month could make him feel special with a kiss on the cheek and a small compliment.

But then Rylee made him feel a lot of things he hadn't felt in a long time. And color him a coward, but that scared him. He knew he wasn't on his last leg, but he also knew that he had a lot of years on her, and most May to December romances he'd witnessed had a habit of turning sour after a couple of years.

He reckoned he'd rather never have something than have it and lose it. Hearing his name called, he shoved aside those thoughts and turned his mind to the business at hand.

*****

Rylee had never taken part in anything like this camp-out. The entire Brickman family, most of the wranglers, Bear or Bobby, as was his real name, and his family loaded up the wagons with food and supplies, tents, and chairs, and headed out across the land.

She'd been given a beautiful mare to ride, and thanks to Ike riding close beside her, she felt safe and at ease. "This is incredible," she said when he stopped at the crest of a hill. The land seemed to stretch forever in every direction. "And it's yours."

"To that low range just beyond the river," he pointed, "And– well as far as you can see in every other direction."

"I'd never leave if this place was mine," she commented. "I'd have my food delivered–no wait, I'd grow it, and after harvest I'd can and freeze, make jam, and-" she paused and laughed. "Well, I'd have to learn, but wow, what a life that would be."

She turned to find Ike smiling at her. "What?"

"You never fail to surprise me, Rylee Monroe. Most city folks find this too remote for their taste."

"Then they definitely don't deserve something like this. They'd just mess it up with concrete and high-rises."

"Amen to that."

"Is that the river we're going to fish in?"

"Yep."

"Can we swim in it?"

"If you're a bear, have at it. The water's probably sixty to sixty-five degrees."

"Okay, that's a bit cold."

"You can still fish."

"I've never done that except deep-sea fishing, and I wasn't keen on that."

"Why not?"

She made a face. "It had something to do with puking my guts out for four hours."

Ike laughed. "I don't think I'd care for that either."

"Oh look, there come the wagons," she said as she checked behind them. "This is like some kind of western adventure. Well, for me, I've never done anything like this."

"Never gone camping?"

"Not in a long time. Have you been to Florida?" Her eyebrows arched dramatically. "If there's water, there are gators and snakes, and I'm not exactly a fan of either. I used to kayak and paddle board until a snake fell out of a tree onto my board. I wouldn't go for a month, and when I finally did, a gator rammed my kayak and turned me over. I nearly had a heart-attack."

"Why not kayak in the ocean?"

"Oh, I tried. A friend who was with me rammed and capsized me, and I ended up getting stung by jellyfish. That wasn't pleasant."

Ike laughed. "I'm starting to think maybe we shouldn't let you fish, you're a magnet for mishap."

She laughed as well. "You may be right, but I reckon there are enough big strong cowboys in this crew to protect me."

"You feel you need protection?"

She smiled at him, and he felt the tingle down to his toes. "If it's the right cowboy, I just might. Know any volunteers?"

"Maybe," he said, and started forward. "Come on."

Once they reached the top of the next hill, Ike stopped and Rylee drew alongside him, stopped, and looked around. "What's that?" she pointed at a ten o'clock position from where they sat on their horses.

"A river?"

"No, on the other side of the hill. It looks like a giant ditch."

"That's where the river used to be."

"Used to be? It just up and moved?"

"We moved it."

"You moved a river?" She gave him an incredulous look. "How is that possible and why would you do such a thing?"

Ike looked out over the valley for a few moments. "See where that big ditch, as you call it, seems to start?"

"Yes."

"Well, back when I was young, in my early twenties, a family who owned that piece of land dammed the river and cut off the water supply to our land, and two other property owners who own adjoining properties.

"My dad and the other men tried to talk to the owner, but he wouldn't listen to reason and basically told us to go to hell. So, dad and the other owners got together, hired an excavation company, and tapped into the underground flow of water. Then, they dug a new trench, wider and deeper, and that became the new river."

"And how did the guy who dammed the river get water after that?"

"He didn't."

Rylee frowned at him. "So, you did the same to him he tried to do to you?"

"Pretty much."

"And how do you feel about that?"

Ike considered the question. "To be honest, I didn't care. The owner, Roy Durning, was a mean old cuss who'd just as soon shoot you as look at you. He beat his kids, put his poor wife in hospital half a dozen times before she got up the gumption to leave, and spent most of what he made on cheap liquor."

"So, you don't think it was wrong?"

"I don't know, Rylee. What would you have done if someone cut off the water supply for thousands of acres of land, just out of spite?"

"That's a good question, and I don't know. What happened to Mr. Durning?"

"He died of liver cancer, and his kids inherited the land, but they couldn't afford the taxes on it, so we bought it from them at above fair market value."

"Well, that was compassionate. What happened to them after that?"

"Don't have a clue."

"Maybe they started new lives and are happy somewhere else."

"Maybe so."

"It sure is beautiful here."

"Indeed, it is. Come on." Ike kicked his horse into a gallop. After a few seconds, he realized Rylee had done the same. It surprised him how quickly she'd caught on to riding. She moved with the horse like she'd been riding her entire life.

And she was pretty darn sexy in that saddle. He almost groaned. Of course, she'd have to learn to ride well. It was one of his secret turn-ons—a woman who could ride. Ike wondered what he'd done to have God send such temptation his way.

Chapter Twenty

Matt sat beside Rylee and rocked over to bump his shoulder against hers. "Still no luck?"

She wrinkled her nose and shook her head. "Wyoming fish hate me."

"Or they're just not biting."

"It's okay, I'm having fun watching."

"Yeah?"

"Yeah," she smiled at him. "You can't tell the family from the employees. It's like you're all one big family."

"In a way, we are."

"That must feel good."

"I guess it does. Funny, but until now I never thought about it. You have a way of making people look at things differently, you know that?"

"Do I?" she shrugged. "Maybe it's because I see it from the eyes of an outsider, and you can't see it any other way than from within."

"Maybe so. I'm glad you help me see it from another perspective. It makes me appreciate it more."

"You should. You and your family are so lucky. You have this beautiful paradise to live and work in, you all love and care for one another, and you never have to be alone unless you just need some space."

"You miss your family, don't you?" Matt looped his arm around her shoulders.

"More than you can imagine," she stared at the water.

"Invite your brother to come for a visit."

"He's deployed."

"Not for forever. Tell him you want to see him. I bet he'll come. Hell, I'll pay for it."

"Oh no, I can afford to pay for his airfare, and I will." She leaned her head against him for a second. "You're a good friend."

"And you're a lousy fisherman," he said, grabbed her pole and tossed it aside.

"Hey!" she protested and then squealed when he stood, grabbed her from behind and marched straight out into the cool water.

Matt reckoned her scream could be heard for miles. She thrashed around, broke loose, and then dove at him. They both went down, and the shock of the cold had him pushing to the surface and gulping in air.

"Oh, it's on," he warned.

"Indeed, it is," she smiled and glanced behind him.

He was a moment too late in looking. Tom grabbed him and into the water they both went. The moment they surfaced, Tom went after Rylee. She squealed and started for shore, but wasn't fast enough. He picked her up in both arms and said, "hang on," then into the water they went.

For the next few minutes, it was a battle. Then Matt noticed Rylee shivering and her lips taking on a blue tint. "Okay, time to get to the fire."

"I got her." Tom snatched Rylee up and carried her to where the campfire was blazing.

"Oh g-g-g-g-g-god, it's cold," she said when he set her on her feet.

"Thomas Brickman!"

Everyone turned at the sound of Georgia's voice, and Tom immediately threw up his hands. "It was Matt. He started it."

"I did not," Matt exclaimed as he stepped up to the fire, squishing water with every step.

"You clods are going to freeze her to death," Georgia scolded. "Get yourself out of those wet clothes and get dry. Rylee, you come with me."

"Ye–ye–yes, ma'am," Rylee complied, and Georgia led her away.

Matt punched Tom in the arm. "Tattletale."

Tom grinned and headed for the tent they were sharing. By the time they were both changed, and had their clothes hanging from sticks driven into the ground near the fire, the smell of cooking beef and roasted corn wafted through the air.

Liz walked over with two cups of coffee. "Sit down and get warm."

A second later, Rylee bounded out of her tent carrying her wet clothes. She stopped, eyed Matt and Tom's wet clothes, dropped her own and started scouring around for sticks.

"Need some help?" Matt yelled.

"No, I can do it." She yelled over her shoulder, then put her hands on her hips for a moment.

"This should be interesting," Tom commented as Ike and Asa took seats by the fire.

A moment later, Rylee ran over to where Bear was cooking. They talked for a minute, then he handed his wife, Cathy, his utensils, and went to the wagon. After rumbling around for a minute, he returned with two stout tent stakes, a piece of rope, and a small sledgehammer.

Rylee gave him a kiss on the cheek, grinned at Ann, then called out to the kids, Benny, and Cathy. She led them to her tent, and as everyone watched, they knotted the rope to each stake and then drove the stakes into the ground.

Cathy ran to fetch Rylee's clothes, and together, they hung the wet articles on the makeshift clothesline. After much cheering and high-fiving, Rylee hugged both kids, and then returned to the fireside.

"Well, I'm impressed," Asa said.

"Thank you, kind sir," she replied, "but I couldn't have done it without my buddies. Right guys?"

Both kids piped up to agree and ran over to sit beside Rylee on the ground, one of either side of her.

"Pull up a stump," Tom suggested.

"I'm fine, thanks." Rylee smiled. "That water was cold, but–" she grinned. "It was fun."

"Did you catch a fish?" Benny asked.

"A whale," Rylee replied.

"Really?" Cathy asked.

"You bet'cha. His name was Matt."

Both kids laughed, and after a moment everyone else joined in, except Matt, who was protesting. "I beg your pardon. Tom is clearly the whale, while I am more like a sleek shark."

"In your dreams, minnow," Tom quipped.

Rylee laughed along with everyone else and glanced over at Ike. He was so handsome when he smiled, and she felt almost star-struck. Their gazes connected and his smile faded, to be replaced by an expression she instinctively recognized. It translated into a feeling that was currently permeating her, making the last of the cold fade.

Desire was powerful, and she'd never realized how powerful it was until this moment. "I could use a hand," Georgia called from the chuck wagon.

"Let me!" Rylee jumped up, relieved to be released from the dominance Ike's gaze had over her.

"Me too!" Benny piped up, followed by his sister. "I'll help."

Rylee took their hands and hurried over. Twenty minutes later, people filled plates with food. She got in line, filled her plate, and walked over to where Ike sat on a log by the fire. "Is that seat taken?"

"It will be when you sit."

Rylee couldn't remember having more fun than sitting around the fire, eating good food, talking, and laughing. It was even fun cleaning up. Once everything was taken care of, it was dark. Bear, Ann, and his parents herded their kids off, leaving the family sitting around the fire.

"This was a good day," Rylee said.

"Yes, it was," Matt agreed.

"You're all lucky, you know," Rylee said. "You can do this whenever you want."

"We should do it more," Georgia agreed.

"You're right," Asa said. "Nothing I like better than snuggling my honey under the stars."

The smile Georgia gave Asa made Rylee long to know what it must feel like to have that kind of enduring love.

After an hour or so, Asa and Georgia called it a night and headed for their tent. Half an hour later, Tom stood, stretched, and yawned. "Good night, folks. Sleep well."

Rylee jumped up and ran to throw her arms around Tom. "Thanks for getting soaked with me."

"Anytime gorgeous." He gave her a kiss on the cheek, then turned and headed for his tent.

213

"Hell, I better turn in and try to get to sleep before he starts snoring," Matt said and stood. He gave Rylee a big hug. "If you get scared, yell?"

"Yeah? You gonna come protect me?"

"No, I'm gonna bring you a stick. I don't figure you know how to shoot."

"What a guy," she rolled her eyes, then smiled. "Sleep well."

"You too. Good night, Dad."

"Good night, son." Ike replied.

"I'm turning in, as well," Liz stood, stretched, then looked at Rylee. "Which bunk do you want?"

"Whichever you don't pick."

"Works for me. Just don't sit on me when you come in."

"I'll pat first," Rylee said with a smile. "Good night."

"Night, Rylee. Night, Daddy."

"Sleep well, sweetheart," Ike responded.

Rylee reclaimed her seat on the log beside Ike and grimaced at the twinge in her back.

"You didn't pull your stitches out, did you?" Ike asked. "It might have been a bit soon for all that tussling in the water."

"No, I don't think so. It was just a twinge. I'm fine."

"Good."

He stared at the fire, and after a minute of silence, she said, "I guess you are all accustomed to going to bed kind of early."

"We typically get up before daylight."

"Oh, yes. I forgot. I'm sorry. Then you should call it a day."

"I'll sit here with you as long as you like."

"That's thoughtful, but no. I've had a wonderful day and I won't ask for more—well, maybe just one more thing."

"What's that?"

"Would you walk me to my tent?"

"Yes, I will."

They rose and strolled to the tent set up for her. She stopped and turned to Ike. "Thank you for today."

"You seemed to have fun."

"I did."

"It looked like Tom and Matt had a good time."

"They're good men, and I think maybe good friends, too. I like them."

"And they're both single."

"Yes, I know."

"And?"

She was quiet for a moment, trying to decide whether to act on what she wanted or let the moment pass. "And this…"

Rylee reached up to put her hand on the back of his neck and pull him down to meet her kiss. For a moment, Ike was tense, and she feared she'd overstepped. Then his arms went around her, and for as long as the kiss lasted, she was aware only of that. His taste and the feel of his arms around her and their bodies pressed together.

When it ended, he didn't release her, and for a moment, just stared down into her eyes. "You're never who I imagine, are you Rylee Monroe?"

"I don't know. Who did you imagine I am?"

"A woman I could kiss and walk away from without regret."

"Am I not that?"

"Not even close. Good night, Rylee. Sleep well."

This time the kiss was sweet and quick, a chaste little pressing of lips. She nodded and turned to open the tent flap. "Good night, Ike. Thanks for giving me a day I'll never forget."

"You're welcome."

She entered the tent and let the flap fall closed behind her, wishing that he had invited her to his tent. But he hadn't. Still, there was that kiss, and that's what she thought about until sleep claimed her.

Chapter Twenty-One

Rylee smelled coffee. She lowered the blanket that was bunched up around her face and realized it was still dark. No one was awake in the middle of the night. She must have dreamed the smell. Then the flap on her tent wafted from the breeze and she caught the scent again.

Between the alluring aroma and the call of nature, it was clear she wasn't going back to sleep. She threw back the covers, grabbed her jacket and slid it on, then shoved her feet into her shoes and grabbed her tissue.

She didn't see anyone when she left the tent, but to make sure, she walked to a stand of trees she'd used earlier as her latrine, relieved herself and then toed a hole in the dirt and buried the tissue.

When she returned to camp, the campfire was blazing. People were standing at the chuck wagon, and someone sat on a log by the fire. She walked over to find Ike sitting on the log with a cup in his hand.

"I didn't figure to see you before noon," he commented.

"Seriously?" she sat down beside him. "It's going to take something more serious than a little gunshot, like a whole lot of sexy, to keep me in bed that long."

Rylee bit back a smile when Ike choked on his coffee. "Need me to pound you on the back?" she asked.

"No," he managed to get the word out, cleared his throat and tried again. "No, I'm fine."

She sniffed the air. "Where can a girl get a cup of that coffee?"

He pointed to the wagon, and she stood. "Want me to get you a refill since I'm headed that way?"

"I wouldn't say no to it."

She held out her hand, and he gave her his mug. Bear and his wife, Ann, were busy prepping for breakfast. "Could I get a cup of coffee?" Rylee asked. "And a refill for Mr. Brickman?"

"Sure thing." Ann grabbed a towel and lifted the big metal pot from the grill over the fire. She refilled Ike's cup and poured one for Rylee. "Cream and sugar?"

"Cream, if you have it. A lot. I like a little coffee with my cream."

Ann chuckled. "Same here. Bear always shakes his head when he sees me fix my coffee."

"It must be one of those manly-man things," Rylee commented. "I take my coffee black and strong enough to walk out of cup."

This time, Ann and Bear laughed. "You want steak for breakfast?" Bear asked.

"God, no. But if you're fixing those to-die-for biscuits you make, I'll gladly relieve you of a couple of those."

"With honey and butter?" Ann asked.

"Oh my god, are you my long-lost sister?" Rylee quipped.

She saw the smile that brought to Ann's face and Bear's as well and wondered if they truly felt like family here, or people who were always on the outside. Just employees.

"That coffee's gonna get cold before you get to the fire."

Rylee turned to see Ike behind her. "You move quiet for a big man. Here you go."

She handed him a cup and just as he lifted it to his lips, realized she'd given him the wrong cup. He found that out soon enough. No sooner had he taken a drink, he made a face. "What in the hell is that?"

"My coffee," Rylee held out his cup. "Trade."

"You sure know how to destroy a good cup of coffee."

She looked back at Ann. "See what I mean? Manly men take their coffee black and strong enough to eat through saddle leather."

Ann put a hand to her face to cover a smile, but Bear chuckled. Rylee looked at Ike to see if he was annoyed, but he was smiling as well. "Always the smart ass."

Rylee shrugged and wandered over to sit on the log by the fire. She listened with half an ear as Ike and Bear talked about the weather, needing to get to the slaughterhouse and get the cow they'd had butchered, and whether the weather was going to stay kind, or they should head back to the ranch before dark.

It didn't sound like an employer and employee conversation. It sounded like a family talk. That pleased and impressed her. Ike seemed to make everyone feel like family.

And that thought, surprising, struck a sour chord inside her. Was he treating her so kindly, and even feigning interest just to be kind?

He walked over and sat down beside her as she stewed over that question. "Something bothering you?"

She shook her head. "Just thinking."

"About?"

Rylee turned her head to look at him. "Are you a tease?"

"Pardon?" She could see the surprise on his face.

"A tease? You know, leading a woman on just to–to be kind or whatever."

"What in the world would make you ask something like that?"

She shrugged and looked at the fire. "I don't know. I guess it's… forget it."

"I'm not sure I can."

"Fine," she glanced at him. "Do you like me?"

"Yes."

"Are you attracted to me?"

"I don't want to have that talk now."

"Do you ever want to have it?"

"I don't know, but I do know this isn't the place or time."

Despite feeling rebuked, she agreed. "You're right. I apologize."

"Just like that? No fussing or histrionics?"

Rylee laughed. "Is that what you think women do when someone disagrees with them?"

"It's what most women do."

"I don't agree with that, but I won't argue."

He shook his head. "There you go, Rylee Monroe, surprising me."

She smiled and then looked behind him at Asa, who was headed their way. "Hey there, handsome," she said and stood. "Have my seat. I've got it warmed up for you."

"That's my girl," Asa grinned, and claimed the place she'd vacated.

"I'm going to see if I can help," Rylee said. "Mr. Asa, I'll bring you some coffee if you want."

"Rylee, if I was single, I'd propose to you."

"And I'd accept," she teased in reply

As she walked away, she heard Asa's voice. "Son, if you don't lay claim to that gal, you're dumb as a sack of rocks."

Rylee bit back a laugh and said a silent thanks to Asa, then walked over to the wagon. "Can I get a coffee for Asa? And then I want to help."

"Seriously?" Ann asked.

"Yes ma'am, put me to work."

For the next hour, Rylee was busy. It was fun. Georgia and Elsie joined in, and it was like a gathering of friends getting together to cook and eat. By the time breakfast was over and everything was cleaned up and put away, the sun was up, and the sky was clear.

"So, what do you want to do this morning, hotshot?" Matt asked.

"Can we go for a ride and maybe more fishing?"

"You know it. And I brought a drone."

"Cool!" She gave him a hug. "Let's do it."

Everyone who wanted to ride saddled up. She insisted on saddling her horse, but Ike helped to make sure it was snug and secure. They headed out with Ike, Matt, Tom, and Asa. Bear stayed behind with Ann, the kids, his parents, Liz and Georgia. They planned on meeting up with everyone at the river at midday.

Matt and Tom rode ahead, leaving Ike, Asa, and Rylee in their dust. "They still act like kids when they get out here," Asa commented.

"Maybe that's a good thing," Rylee commented. "We all need to cut loose now and then, set aside all the adulting and responsibility for a little while and just be, don't you think?"

"You're a smart cookie," Asa grinned and looked over at Ike. "Whaddaya say, son. Got it in you?"

"Ask me that when you catch me," Ike said and kicked his mount.

Rylee watched him take off and then Asa as he kicked his horse into a gallop. She wasn't sure she was ready for it, but figured she might as well give it a go and did the same.

At first it was scary, but that quickly transformed into exhilaration. She laughed and urged her horse to go faster.

Just as she caught up with Asa, she heard the crack of a gunfire. Dust exploded on the ground in front of Asa's horse, and it reared. "Get on the ground!" Ike yelled and headed back for them.

Rylee felt like her heart was now lodged in her throat. Trying to control her fear, she quickly dismounted. By the time her feet were on the ground, Asa had dismounted.

"What the hell's going on here?" He shouted as more shots rang out.

Oh God, not again. Fear shot through her, making her stomach lurch. Was this place trying to kill her? Another shot sounded. This time, she watched in horror as blood spurted from her horse's neck. It neighed, wobbled, and fell.

Rylee started for it, but Asa grabbed her arm. "Help me get him on the ground." Between the two of them, they got his horse down on the ground and, just as he knelt beside it, there were more shots.

Rylee was terrified they were going to be killed. Without considering the wisdom of her actions, she dove at Asa, getting between him and the bullets, and as they went down, she felt something tear through her left arm. Asa grunted, and blood spewed from his shoulder.

With a scream, Rylee pushed him down flat on the ground and lay on top of him. "Ike!" she screamed. "Ike!"

Within seconds, Ike was beside them. "How bad?" he asked.

"It went clean through," Asa said. "But it's bleeding like a son of a gun."

That's when Ike noticed Rylee's arm. "You're bleeding, too."

She ignored his comment. She was so scared she couldn't feel any pain and at that moment, all she wanted was to get out of there and get Asa help. "We have to get Asa medical attention."

Ike pulled out his phone. "Jason, bring the chopper and call the police." He proceeded to tell whoever Jason was, their location and then pocketed his phone. "Help's on the way."

"Who's Jason?" she asked.

"Pilot."

"Oh."

"We're sitting ducks," Asa commented.

"Not for long," Ike nodded off to his left and Rylee looked to see Matt and Tom tearing toward them.

Before they even reached them, both men dismounted. Matt was the first man off his horse, and by the time Tom grabbed a rifle from his saddle and slapped his horse to get it moving, Matt was flattened out on the ground, looking through the scope of a rifle.

The gunfire started again, but this time in Matt and Tom's direction. They returned fire and then everything went silent.

It felt like an eternity as they lay there, waiting for more shots to be fired or help to come. Rylee took off her jacket. "Help me," she said to Ike.

"Do what?"

"Get out of this shirt. I can use it to help stop the bleeding."

Between the two of them, they removed her shirt. She wadded up her jacket and tied it around the shirt she'd folded, to make a makeshift compress for Asa's shoulder.

"Here," Ike peeled off his jacket. "You can't go around like that."

"Thanks," Rylee slid on the jacket and zipped it closed to cover herself.

"How's your arm?" Ike asked.

"Hurts like hell."

"You saved me, Missy," Asa said in a decidedly weaker than normal voice.

"Then you stay with me," she replied.

"You seem to be making a habit of saving people in this family," Ike said. "And getting shot."

"I'm starting to wonder if this place is trying to get rid of me," she replied, trying to stem the way her body was trembling.

"Not as long as I draw breath," Asa said.

She put her hand on his back. "If only you were single, Mr. Asa."

"Well, you can have the next best thing."

"Oh?"

"Yeah, Ike's available."

Rylee smiled despite the pain, realizing that Asa was trying to turn her mind away from the fear. "I'll give that some thought."

That's when she looked at Ike, and to her surprise, saw something in his eyes she hadn't expected.

Rage.

"He's going to make it," she whispered to him.

"I'm going to find whoever is doing this and rain hell on him."

Of that, Rylee had no doubt at all.

Chapter Twenty-Two

As soon as the doctor left the room, Rylee slid off the bed and started looking around for the jacket she had on when she was brought into the emergency room. She found it in a big plastic bag with her name on it, along with her shoes and her iWatch.

She was just putting on her shoes when the door opened, and Ike walked in. "Is Mr. Brickman okay?"

"Yes, he's doing well. The bullet passed through without hitting anything vital, but he lost a good bit of blood, so they cleaned and sewed him up, put him on an IV and are keeping him overnight. Mom's already set up with a recliner and the TV remote and plans on staying with him."

"Thank God." She fastened her watch on her wrist.

"And you're okay?" Ike asked.

Rylee glanced at him, and it surprised her to notice the concern on his face. "I am. Three stitches, and they redid several, I pulled loose, but I'm free to go."

"Well, lucky for you, I'm here to give you a ride."

"Thank you. Do you think I could see your parents before we leave?"

"Don't see why not."

He escorted her down the hall, keeping his hand on the middle of her back. Rylee noticed several nurses glancing their way and wondered if they were thinking that they'd love to be in her shoes.

She almost laughed. Her shoes weren't enviable. Since she'd been here, she'd failed to get a definite answer about what happened to the missing data, had been shot twice and was falling in love with a man who had no intention of getting romantically involved with her.

Ike stopped at a closed door, tapped, and after a moment Rylee heard Georgia call out, "Come in."

He opened the door for Rylee. The moment she stepped in, Georgia engulfed her in a tight hug. "Thank you."

They both cried a little, and when Georgia released her, Asa spoke up. "Got one of those hugs for me?"

"Always." Rylee hurried to the bed when he sat propped up and climbed onto the bed to lay her head gently on his good shoulder. "I don't think I could stand it if something happened to you, Mr. Asa."

"Thanks to you, I'll be right as rain in a few days," he kissed her forehead, then looked over at Ike. "You best take this girl home and make sure she's looked after until your mama and I get home."

"I will, Pop."

"Then get a move on. It's getting late."

"Is there anything you need?" Rylee got off the bed and addressed Georgia. "We could come in the morning with fresh clothes and some decent coffee."

"Oh, that would be wonderful. Thank you."

"I'm glad to help. Now, we'll get out of here and let you both rest. If you need anything call, okay?"

"You know we will." Georgia walked over to give her another hug. "I won't ever forget what you've done for this family, child. You've saved two people I love. Whether you wanted it, you're my family now."

Rylee tried to push back the tears, but there was no stopping them. It'd been so long since she'd had a family, and the loneliness was often more than she felt she could bear. To be considered family was the highest honor she could imagine, and the answer to a prayer.

"Thank you," she whispered. "That means more than anything to me."

"And to me," Georgia added and stepped back. "Ike, make sure she gets something to eat."

"I will. Good night mom," he hugged Georgia, then took Asa's hand. "Behave."

Asa chuckled. "Not a chance."

Ike grinned and gestured to Rylee. "Ready to go?"

"Yes."

Rylee kept her gaze on the floor until they were outside. Then she stopped, looked up, and took a long breath. Ike put his hand on her shoulder. "You sure you're okay?"

"Yes, I just…" she trailed off, not sure how to put what she felt into words, and finally decided it wasn't the place or time, so instead she finished with, "I just wonder if Wyoming hates me."

"Well, when you go around saving people, you put yourself in harm's way."

"You would've done the same thing."

"This isn't about me." He pointed to his truck in the parking lot and took her arm as they started walking again.

"Why was someone shooting at us, Ike? What would make someone want to kill us?"

"I don't have an answer, but I'm damn sure going to figure it out."

She nodded, and when he opened the door for her, she climbed into the truck. All the way to the ranch, she ran through the events of the day in her mind, and when they arrived, she got out and leaned against the truck, staring up at the sky.

"There must be a reason," she said. "Did you jilt someone's sister? Beat them in some equine competition? Outrun, outfight, outsmart or outfuck them?"

"Damn, Rylee, you and that mouth."

She waved a dismissive hand at him. "You've heard worse, but seriously? What would make someone do something like that?"

"Like I said, I don't know. When you've been in business as long as my family, you're bound to make enemies. Most of them are more competitors than real enemies. Some people let a defeat or loss make them bitter. Maybe that's the case here. I'll talk to Pop when he gets home and see if he has any ideas."

"And until then?"

"Until then, we all need to be mindful and stay sharp."

"Do you think whoever it is will try again?"

Ike shrugged, and for a few minutes they were both quiet, staring up at the sky. When he spoke again, it was with a question she wasn't sure she wanted to answer.

"Why did you cry when Mom said you're family now?"

Rylee looked at him and sighed. "Can we sit?"

"Inside or out?"

"Either."

"Let's go in where it's warm."

They went inside, and he gestured to the couch in front of the fireplace in the spacious family room. There were already embers, and after he added new logs, he sat beside her on the couch. "So?"

The few minutes it took him to tend the fire gave her time to consider her answer. She opened her mouth to give a glib or not quite true answer, but then she looked at him. There was no way she could look him in the eyes and lie.

Scared this might be what would have him asking her to leave or turning his back on her, she took a deep breath. "You're lucky.

You still have both your parents and three children, and a ranch full of people who care about you.

"When my parents died, I felt—cut adrift, untethered and alone. I didn't even get to have a funeral. Their bodies were never recovered. It was like—like they just disappeared, and my family disappeared with them. Rayce didn't come home because there was nothing he could do, so it was just me that was left to settle up their estate, clean out their house and–"

Emotion overwhelmed her, and she lowered her head. "I never knew how lonely life could be, or how easy it was to be alone, no matter how many people are around. It took a year before I could go a day without crying. Now there's just this empty place." She looked at him and put her hand over her heart. "And today when your mother said–when she said I was family, it was the first time I felt like someone cared."

Nothing could have surprised her more than to have him gather her into his arms. "She's not the only one who cares."

"No?"

"Everyone here has already fallen in love with you."

"No everyone," she pulled free and gazed into his eyes.

"Rylee, I–"

"Don't. Don't put me off again. Just tell me straight out."

Ike released her, stood, and walked over to the fireplace. He put one hand on the mantel as he gazed into the fire. "If you were older or I–"

"Oh please!" She jumped up and crossed the room to take hold of his arm and turn him toward her. "Would you look at me please?"

It took a moment, but he complied. "Age doesn't matter, Ike. At least not to me. Are you ashamed to be seen with a younger woman?"

"No, it's not that."

"Then what is it? You can't believe people would perceive you as someone who could only find a younger woman because of money?"

"Oh, they'd think it."

"Well, who cares? I don't care about your land or money. I can make my own way in life and don't need someone to provide for me. But I do want..."

"What? What do you want?"

"I want you."

"Why? Why not Matt or Tom or any of a hundred young men who'd jump at the chance to call you their girl?"

"Well, first, I'm no longer a girl and second, what causes any of us to be attracted to someone? There's looks and you score high in that category. Then there's personality and while you can be all business when you need to, you can also be a lot of fun. You're kind and you care about people and the land and you're honest and seem to be fair, and you're sexy and it's for damn sure you can curl a woman's toes with a kiss. To condense it all down—you're hot and you turn me on, and I enjoy being with you, simply being—talking or riding or dancing or whatever, I don't care. I just like being with you."

There was a long silence, and before he spoke, she knew he was going to shoot her down. "I like you too. And yes, I'm attracted to you—more than I'm comfortable with, and I wish I could say to hell with the age difference, but it bothers me."

Rylee nodded. "Okay, thanks for your honesty. Now, if you'll excuse me, I think I'm going to turn in."

She didn't wait for him to say more. She simply turned and hurried from the room. Once inside the guest room, she closed the door, kicked off her shoes, and then peeled out of her clothes.

Compared to the toasty warmth of the family room, her room felt cool, but she didn't mind. That didn't matter much at the moment. She needed to shower and get the hospital smell off her.

Just as she gathered her clothes to put them into her dirty clothes bag, the bedroom door opened so fast, it banged back against the wall, framing Ike in the opening.

"Wha–?" She never got the word out. In two long steps, he was in front of her, grabbing the dirty clothes to toss them aside. His eyes moved down her body and back up to lock with hers.

"I still have a problem with the age difference, but…"

With that, he took her into his arms and kissed her. Rylee wound her arms around his waist and ran her hands up his back, pressing tighter to him. When the kiss ended, she was breathing faster, and no longer felt the least bit cool.

"I was going to shower the hospital off me. Want to join?"

Ike's response was to toe off one boot, then reach down to yank off the other. By the time he straightened, she was working to unfasten his belt. Rylee moved backwards, headed for the bathroom as she continued. And by the time she reached in to start the shower, he was naked and running his hands over her body.

Ike picked her up and stepped into the shower with her. She wound her legs around his waist. "Fair warning. If this is a mistake, then I'll make it worth the regret I feel later. I'm going to take my time with you, Rylee, and satisfy every thought I've had since I met you of the things I'd do to you if we ever got together. So, if you want to back out, now's the time."

"Not a chance."

"So be it," he claimed her with a kiss that made all thoughts of missing data, getting shot and feeling alone vanished. Now there was only him. Only them.

And that was all that mattered.

Chapter Twenty-Three

Ike woke when he felt movement. A moment later, Rylee rolled over, throwing one arm over his chest and a leg across his, pressing herself against his side. Were it not for the fact that he felt she needed sleep, he would give into temptation, push her onto her back and have her again.

He was pretty sure he'd not be able to stop thinking about their night for a long time. Maybe ever. Ike had been with his share of women, but he'd never been with anyone that made him feel the way she did. Rylee could be submissive and surrender to whatever he wanted, and she could be demanding, taking control of their lovemaking. Both were exciting. He wasn't sure how to walk away. If he were honest, he'd admit he didn't want to.

He probably should, but the thought of it pained him. He'd probably never meet another woman like her, and probably never feel about another woman the way he felt about her. Tonight, he'd finally accepted he was falling in love with her. Still, was it wise to pursue a relationship or would it be smart to end it now?

Heck, she might wake up, look at him and tell him that was nice, but now it was out of her system. That would sure sting, but he guessed it would at least release him from the responsibility of having to decide. He spent the next half hour coming up with what he'd say to her, trying to find the right words. When he glanced at her, it surprised him to find her watching him.

"No," she said.

"No what?"

"No, you can't get up and leave yet. No, you can't pretend like it didn't happen, or you didn't enjoy it, or you don't want it to happen again. And no, you can't say it didn't mean anything, because I know it did."

It bothered him that she was right. "So, if I can't do any of those things, what can I do?"

"You can make love to me."

"Make love?"

Rylee reached over to put her hand on the side of his face. "I waited my entire life to fall in love, Ike, and now I have, so I can never again merely have sex with you, and I'm hoping the same is true for you."

Hearing her say she was in love with him delivered a punch a hundred times more potent than the one he'd experienced the first time he looked into her eyes, and Ike realized right then that no matter what he came up with as a reason to walk away, he wouldn't.

Because, like it or not, he was in love with her.

*****

Matt rapped on his father's door, feeling a little concerned. His dad never slept in, and it was closing in on half-past eight. When there was no answer, Matt cracked open the door and called out. "Dad?"

Getting no answer, he glanced in. The room was empty. That sent a jolt of concern through him. He headed downstairs and found Bear in the kitchen. "Did Dad ever come down for breakfast?"

"Not yet."

"Damn. He's not in his room, so–"

"Because he's in Rylee's," Bear's mother, Elsie, turned from where she stood cleaning a window.

"He's what?"

"In Rylee's room. I was going to check if she needed fresh towels, but the door was closed, and I could hear them."

"Talking?"

"No."

"Then–" Matt noticed the expression on Elsie's face and glanced from her to Bear. "Are you serious?"

"Apparently, that little firebrand got under his skin," Elsie commented.

"Well, I'll be damned."

"Be damned about what?"

Everyone looked, and Ike stopped just inside the kitchen. "Someone want to tell me why you're all standing there gaping at me like I just grew another ear?"

Matt glanced at Rylee, who stepped in behind Ike, and she grinned. Matt then looked at his dad. "Nothing, dad. Chief Rogers dropped off some keys for Rylee and two cell phones that were pretty banged up. He said he was going to take them to No Limits, but since he promised to bring the keys to her here, he figured he'd deliver the phones at the same time."

"What keys and phones?" Ike glanced at Rylee, who'd scooted around him and was pouring two cups of coffee.

"The keys to Brent's house and his and Dennis's cell phones. I'm going to get my hardware guy, Kyle, to help me break in and see if we can salvage the data."

"Why?"

Rylee answered as she carried the two mugs of coffee across the room. "Because if Brent is involved in the missing footage, as I suspect, there's a better-than-average chance he communicated with whoever he was going to sell the footage before he died."

Ike nodded and accepted the mug. "Thanks, and that's a smart move."

"I'm a smart girl," she said and winked.

"You sure are," Matt agreed. "Do you want to get started on that today?"

"Yes, I do."

"Need a ride? I have something on the books with the forestry service, but I can see if I can reschedule."

"No, absolutely not. I won't interfere with your work. Maybe I can borrow a car or get someone to drive my car here and–"

"I'll take you," Ike interrupted.

"Are you sure it won't interfere with your day?"

"I'm sure."

"Well thank you," she smiled and looked at Matt. "Problem solved, but thanks for always being willing to be my hero."

"Looks like you've got yourself a new one," he teased.

Rylee grinned. "Now wouldn't that be something?"

"Enough, you two," Ike said, with no real heat in his tone. "What time do you want to leave?"

"Whenever it's good for you," Rylee answered.

"How about we head over around eleven? I have a Cattleman's Association meeting at noon at the Eatery. I can drop you off and meet you at No Limits when I'm done."

"Sounds perfect. That gives me time to see if I can bribe Tom into letting me ride for a bit."

"I don't think you'll have any problems convincing him," Matt said. "I'll see you all later."

Rylee hurried to give him a hug. "Be safe and have a great day."

"See you this evening, son." Ike added, finished his coffee, and carried the cup to the sink. "Bear, Elsie, when you finish up today, I want your family to take a couple of days off. Our camping trip cut into your weekend, and you deserve some downtime."

"Are you sure?" Bear asked.

"I am."

"Thanks. Ann's been bugging me about painting the kids' bedrooms, and I can get most of that done tomorrow while they're in school. It'll be a nice surprise.

"And I'll help," Elsie added.

"Thanks, mom, and thanks again, Mr. Brickman."

"It's the least I can do. Now, if you'll all excuse me, I have some things to tend to before we head to town."

"And I'm going to go bug Tom," Rylee hurried to wash out her cup. "Oh, Bear, I almost forgot. I heard from my boss and No Limits will be happy to donate to the school computer fund. In fact, he said if I wanted to make the donation from the operation here, he'd approve a twenty-thousand-dollar contribution. I'd like to match that amount."

"Are you serious? Ann will be over the moon. Thanks, Rylee."

"What are friends for?" She smiled. "See you when you get back from your time off. Enjoy, okay?"

"You know it."

"Great. And you too, Mrs. Elsie."

"Thanks, Rylee. You have a good day."

"I'm sure going to try."

With that, she headed out of the house. Once outside, she stopped, tilted her face up, and smiled at the sky. "I wish you were here to meet him, Mom and Dad. He's such a remarkable man. Maybe you already know that. I sure hope so. And I hope you know I miss you every day. I love you. Always and forever."

As she started walking toward the barn, it occurred to her that this was the first time she'd spoken with her parents or thought about them without feeling the need to burst into tears. This time, she could picture them in her mind, see the smiles and love they had for her on their faces. For the first time, she could remember them without wanting to hurl herself off a bridge or crawl into a dark hole and hide.

The reason for that was Ike. He hadn't come right out and said it, but she felt it in his touch and saw it in his eyes. He cared for her. For the first, and she suspected, only time in her life, she was in love, and that opened her heart finally to happiness.

*****

Ike watched her walking down the drive, looking out over the land. She spotted him and a smile came on her face. Ike was certain no one had ever looked at him the way she did. Not his girlfriends in high school, not his wife or the women he'd had casual relationships with since his wife left. Rylee looked at him like he was something special.

"I thought you had things to do," she said as she drew near.

"I do."

"And yet, here you stand—doing what?"

"Watching you walk."

She smiled and stopped in front of him. "Careful, you're starting to sound like you're flirting with me."

"Do you want me to flirt with you?"

"I want you to do a lot of things with me."

Ike took hold of her wrist and reeled her into his arms. "Where do you want to start?"

Rylee wound her arms around his neck. "How about a kiss, right here in front of God and the whole ranch?"

His answer was to comply. When the kiss ended, she smiled up at him. "I'm going to be wanting more of that."

"Just whistle, sweetheart."

Rylee laughed. "You may regret that."

"I doubt it."

"So, is Tom available?"

"No, he's out chasing strays with some wranglers. I'm available if you want to ride."

The look she gave him stirred his blood, and her words added fuel to that fire. "Oh, I most definitely want to ride."

"Horses?"

"That too, but since I need to change before we head for town, I thought I should take a shower, and you know, you conserve water if you shower together."

"I knew you were going to be trouble."

"Is that a yes?"

"You bet'cha."

"Then let's get to it, big guy."

Ike laughed in delight, offered her hand and, with hers firmly in his, headed for the house.

Chapter Twenty-Four

Rylee checked the time as they reached the town limits. "Why don't you drop me at my condo, and I'll drive over to Brent's. If you take me there, you'll be late for your meeting."

"You don't mind driving yourself?"

"Heck, no." Rylee reached over and gave Ike's leg a squeeze. "I want to find something that will point the police in the right direction, so they can stop whoever is trying so hard to hurt and kill people."

"I hope you can, but remember, it's not your job to find the killer."

"I know, but I can do things they can't, and I want to help."

"You're a heck of a woman, Rylee Monroe."

"And you're the man of my dreams, Ike Brickman."

They both froze, and she couldn't help wondering who was more surprised. She hadn't intended to blurt out those words, but now they couldn't be unspoken. "I'm sorry. I shouldn't have–"

"I have feelings for you

She looked at Ike. "What?"

"I have feelings for you.

"You do?"

"Yes."

"I–I–oh–I–are you messing with me?"

"Every chance I get, but I mean it. I didn't want to, but it happened anyway."

"And does that make you unhappy?" She wasn't sure how he felt about that sudden declaration.

"No. In fact, it's liberating. I was scared people would talk— look at that old fool with that young woman. And they might, but I no longer care."

"Me either," she assured him. "I won't let them pee on my happiness."

Ike laughed. "Good for you, and I'm with you."

"I think I may have to tell someone," she admitted.

"Why?"

"Because I'm the geek girl who was always too tall, too smart or too something for the cute boys, and now I'm in love with the sexiest man in Wyoming."

"I don't know about that last part, but you tell whoever you want," he pulled in beside her SUV. "I'll meet you at your office when the meeting is over."

"Okay," she unbuckled her seat belt and scooted over to kiss him. "Thank you."

"You're welcome. Drive safe."

"I will. See you later."

She hopped out, unlocked her car, and put her messenger bag on the passenger seat. Then, with a wave to Ike, she backed out and headed for the address of the house where Brent and Dennis had lived.

Rylee sang along with the music she streamed to her car from her phone as she drove. When she reached the house, she parked and sat there for a few seconds. She didn't understand why, but suddenly she was loathed to enter the house.

"Don't be silly," she scolded herself as she got out of the car. "It's not like it's haunted." She marched to the door, but stopped as she inserted the key, overwhelmed by a memory.

She'd put it off for two weeks, despite having made the drive nearly every day. Today she made it as far as the front door before chickening out.

Everyone told her she needed to get it over with so she could move on. She thought they were morons. How the hell did you move on from killing your parents? No matter how many people told her it wasn't her fault, she felt it was.

And she knew that once she stepped foot into their home, she was going to be destroyed. She'd cried a river and hadn't slept a full night since she got the news, and it wasn't getting one bit easier. How was touching their things, smelling them, and listening to the echoes of memories going to make anything better?

Rylee pulled herself back from the memory and swiped at her eyes. She'd finally gotten through going into her parents' house. She could certainly do this. So, with a deep breath, she turned the key and opened the door.

It was easier than she imagined. Was that because she only knew Brent casually? She didn't take time to ponder the question, but set to work going through the place. The only thing she found was Brent's Macbook and Dennis's iPad. She took both with her, made sure the house was locked, and headed for her office.

Once there, she went straight to her office and called out for Kyle and Jack. Kyle was the first into her office. "What's up?"

Rylee gestured to the Macbook and iPad as she pulled the two cell phones from her messenger bag. "We need to break into all these."

"Break into what?" Jack asked as he entered.

She pointed to her desk. "The phones were recovered from Brent's car. The Macbook and iPad came from his house. I need to get into all of them."

"Can I ask why?" Kyle asked.

"You won't like it," Jack replied.

"You already know?"

"I think I do. Rylee?"

She glanced at Kyle. "You know Jack and I have gone through the system, and we both believe someone who works here deliberately erased the missing data."

"Are you kidding? Who would do that?"

"Brent."

"What the hell? Do you hear what you're saying?"

"I do. The information you all gave me painted a picture of a man who suddenly altered his behavior and patterns. Since Brent had autism, he never varied his routine. It wasn't in his nature and would have been upsetting to him. But he did, and something had to have forced him to make such a drastic change.

"The fact that the data was erased without leaving a trail tells us it had to be an inside job."

"You can't know that."

"She can," Jack argued. "I didn't realize until she walked me through it, but there are enough landmines in the system to trip up anyone who wasn't aware of their existence. Without knowledge of where they were and how to avoid them, the system would have locked up when someone tried to tamper with it."

"So naturally, you point a finger at a dead man?"

Rylee could tell it upset Kyle, so she tried to ease the tension by speaking in a calm tone. "Your information was a piece of the puzzle. So was the wrapper for a memory card I found in Brent's desk. I couldn't figure out why he'd left it there. He was, by nature, a tidy person.

"If he'd been in a hurry, he might have tossed it into the drawer without ever considering someone other than him would find it."

"That's not proof."

"No, it's not. But there's more. I checked another of the cameras and there's footage of the Caldwell boy's death."

"Seriously?"

"Yes. I purchased software to enhance the images, and we know he was hit by a black pickup truck, driven by a man with a beard, wearing a baseball cap. Also, on the back window of the truck was an unusual sticker.

"Matt Brickman and his grandfather were piloting drones the day of Brent's death, and he found footage that shows a black truck following Brent's car—one with no plates and the same symbol on the window."

"Shit," Kyle sat down in one of the chairs in front of her desk. "And you think–"

"That if we can get into his computer and phone, we can figure out if he spoke, texted or emailed with someone about the footage."

"And if he did?"

"Then we give the information to the police and hope they can find the person responsible for Donny Caldwell's death, and maybe Brent's as well."

"You think maybe he was run off the road?"

"It's possible, but only speculation at this point. So, what I need from you is your expertise. I want to get into these devices and see what there is to find."

"Then let's get to the control center and get to it," Kyle stood.

"That's my guy," Rylee smiled and looked at Jack. "Are you in?"

"Are you kidding? Lead the way."

She grabbed the phones while Kyle picked up the laptop and tablet, and they all went into the control center. Within minutes, they were set up and ready. And then Rylee lost track of time, as she often did when engaged in a tricky project.

"Rylee?" Lynda's voice from the door had Rylee turning around.

"Mr. Brickman is here."

Rylee checked the time. "Damn, I didn't realize how long we've been here. Tell him to come on back. Guys, I'm going to make a copy of the photo we found on the iPad, and then we're going to call it a day. I want all this stuff locked into the safe."

"You sure you want us to stop?" Kyle asked. "I think we're close to breaking into this phone."

"Yeah, I'm sure. We'll pick back up tomorrow."

"You're the boss."

Just then, Ike entered the room. "You done?"

"Almost. Give me two minutes."

As soon as Rylee copied the photo and texted to the Chief and herself, with a note on where she found it, they gathered all the devices and placed them in the safe. "Okay, guys, I'll see you in the morning, and we'll get back to it. Thanks for the help."

"You bet," Jack replied. "But aren't you supposed to be recuperating?"

"Yeah, as in work from home?" Kyle added.

"I'm fine, thanks. See you tomorrow."

She then turned to Ike. "Ready when you are."

He gestured for her to precede him, and they left the office. Once outside, he stopped. "Do you want to take your car back to your condo?"

"Oh, well, I guess. But I plan on coming back tomorrow and hate to ask you to drive me."

"I don't mind."

"Are you sure?"

"Absolutely."

"Okay, great."

It took less than ten minutes to drive her car home and grab some more clothes. She tossed her small carry-on bag in the back seat of the double-cab truck and climbed into the passenger seat beside Ike.

"Did you find anything?" he asked as he pulled out to head to the ranch.

"So far, nothing. No, I take that back. We found a photo on the iPad belonging to Brent's partner, Dennis. It was of Brent standing outside, talking with a man with short hair, a long beard, sunglasses, and a baseball cap."

"Like the man in the video?"

"Yes."

"Do you think it's the same man?"

"I do, but I have nothing to substantiate that. There was nothing on his laptop."

"What about the phones?"

"They're pretty damaged, but I think we can get them operational. It's just going to take time."

"Most things do. I need to stop by the feed store if you don't mind."

"It's fine with me."

"And I promised Jim Jamieson I'd swing by his ranch and have a look at a bull he just bought and wants to breed. He probably won't be there, but his son, John, will."

"Again, fine with me."

"You sure are agreeable."

"Well, why wouldn't I be? It's a beautiful day, and I get to spend some time with the best-looking man in Brickton, looking at bulls and going to the feed store. I've never been to one. Can I go inside?"

Ike laughed. "I don't see why not."

"Well, all righty then."

Rylee found the feed store charming, and while Ike did business, she struck up a conversation with the owner's wife, who worked there alongside him. By the time they left, she knew the family's history, all about their children and their new grandchild, and heard a lot of gossip about Ike.

When they got back into the truck, she teased him about all the hearts he'd broken. He took it good naturedly, and they headed on to their next stop. The new calves she spotted in the pasture enchanted Rylee. She stood at the fence talking to and petting them as Ike spoke with John.

When they finally left, she realized how late it was. "Hey, what do you say about me treating you to an early supper at The Eatery?"

"If that's what you want, but I'm betting Bear cooked and has supper in the fridge, waiting to be warmed up."

"Oh, I didn't think about that. And besides, I want to check on your dad. He was supposed to come home today. Matt said he was going to pick them up."

"He did. He called while we were in the feed store. Dad and mom are at the main house, so you can see them when we get home."

"Oh good, I love them. And I love Bear's cooking. I'm still not accustomed to having someone do the cooking. And I'm afraid I'm going to get spoiled and then it'll suck when I go back to the condo."

"Then don't go."

"Pardon?"

"You heard me. We have plenty of room and everyone loves having you there."

"Everyone?"

He reached over and gave her leg a squeeze. "Yes, everyone."

Rylee was thrilled but also scared. "What if you get tired of me?"

"What if I don't?"

She smiled. "Well, I like to be optimistic, so… I'll think about it."

Just then a sound like a pop had them both looking, him into the rear-view mirror and her out of the side window. "What was that?" she asked.

"Sounded like a gun."

"What would someone be shooting at out here on the road?"

"Sound travels. It could be someone scaring off a coyote, or shooting a raccoon getting in their trash."

"And why is the truck bumping?"

"Shit." Ike glanced in the rear-view and side mirrors before pulling over onto the side of the road. "That sound might have been a tire being punctured."

"By what?" Rylee suddenly had a bad feeling, and when Ike opened his door, she reached for him. "Let's just call someone. Stay here with me."

"It'll be fine, sweetheart. It's just a flat tire. While I take care of it, call Matt and tell him we're on our way."

"Okay," Rylee watched him get out and walk around to the back of the truck, then she pulled out her phone. Just as Matt answered, she heard another pop. Rylee crammed the phone in her back pocket, opened her door, and got out. One look and she screamed.

Chapter Twenty-Five

"It's okay," Ike motioned to her. "Come on, it's okay."

She hurried to him, and he pulled her behind him. Rylee was shaking with fear as Ike addressed the man in the ball cap who held a rifle pointed at them. "Look, Mister, we have no quarrel with you, so why don't you just back on out and we'll change this tire and be on our way."

"Fuck you, Brickman," the man replied in a gravely tone.

Rylee screamed when he lifted the rifle. She tried to get in front of Ike, but wasn't fast enough. The boom of the gun seemed to coincide with Ike stumbling back. He collided with her, fell, and hit his head on the back bumper of the truck.

"You asshole!" Rylee yelled at the gunman and flung herself down beside Ike. He was bleeding from a long trench on the right side of his head. She was relieved the bullet had grazed him, but scared because he was unconscious.

"Get up!"

Rylee ignored the man and patted Ike's face gently. "Ike? Can you hear me? Ike, it's me. Wake up. Please wake-"

She screamed and dug at the hand tangled in her hair, dragging her away from Ike. The man kicked her in the back hard enough to make spots dance in front of her eyes and oxygen to explode from her lungs. Rylee dug her fingernails into his hand and as soon as she had breath again, started screaming.

"Shut the fuck up!" he slung her around, and she landed face first on the asphalt. She could feel the abrasions on her face and swiped at it, feeling grime and wetness. A quick look told her she was bleeding. That didn't matter. She would survive. From where she lay, she could see Ike. He still wasn't moving. She had to get him help.

Hoping it would buy her time, she lay unmoving on the road. Her assailant marched over and kicked her in the ribs. Rylee howled and tried to roll away, but the man grabbed hold of her arm and hauled her to her feet.

"Move," he shoved her toward the opposite side of the road.

"We need to get him help," she argued, but started walking, albeit as slowly as possible and affecting a limp.

"Let the fucker die. It's what he deserves."

Rylee realized she wasn't going to be able to reason with the man. She had to come up with another way. That's when she remembered her phone in her back pocket. Was Matt still on the line? Praying he was, she started talking. "Where are we going? I'm not all that familiar with the area yet, but I don't remember any houses or farms around here. Is there some rule about owning livestock this close to town? What are we, ten miles from town, twelve?"

"Shut up."

She complied, hoping she'd given Matt enough of a message and glad she'd driven out this way before she was hurt to map out a biking course. The man shoved her again, and she stumbled.

When she righted herself, she made a sound, hoping it sounded like she was in pain, and then hobbled. If nothing else, maybe she could slow him down and an idea of how to escape would come to mind.

That wasn't the case. He just got behind her, shoved, and kept on until they entered a stand of trees where a black truck was parked. That's when Rylee panicked and tried to run. She made it almost back to the road when the man caught up and tackled her.

They rolled around on the ground with her screaming, kicking, and thrashing to keep him off her and him raining blows on her and trying to keep her from getting away. Just as she thought he was tiring, he sat on her abdomen and wrapped both hands around her neck.

She bucked, twisted, dug at his hands with her fingernails, trying to dislodge him. Spots danced in front of her eyes, her lungs screamed for air, and her muscles weakened. Rylee had just enough time to wonder if this was how she was going to die before everything went black.

*****

Ike woke with a jerk, shocked to find himself on the ground. When he tried to sit, a pain shot through his head, making him reach up. He bit back a groan when he touched his head and pulled his hand back. His fingers were bloody.

Moving slowly, he pushed into a sitting position and looked around. "Rylee?" There was no answer. The jolt of alarm sent a shot of adrenaline through him, and he got to his feet. "Rylee?"

She was nowhere to be found. Ike was close to panic. Whoever shot him had taken her. But why? He was about to get into the truck and head for town before he remembered the flat tire. So instead, he called Matt. There was no answer, so he called Tom. Tom answered on the first ring.

"Dad? Thank God, where are you?"

"Something's happened."

"We know. Rylee was on the phone with Matt, and he heard you telling someone you didn't have any fight with him, so you'd change your tire and be on the way. Then a man's voice saying fuck you and Rylee screaming. Are you okay?"

"He shot, but the bullet just grazed my head. I lost consciousness when I fell and when I woke, the man and Rylee were gone. As soon as I change this tire, I'm headed to town to get the police. Is Matt still monitoring her call?"

"Yes, but it went silent a few minutes ago."

"You lost signal?"

"No, there was a lot of screaming and noise and then it just went silent except for bumps and thumps and the sound of doors slamming and an engine starting."

"Jesus. He has her. Call dad, get the wranglers, load up my horse and meet me on state road 32 at the eleven-mile marker. We'll start the search there."

"You sure you're fit to ride?"

"I'll survive, just do it, son. We have to find her."

"On it. See you soon."

Ike ended that call and placed another. Joe barely got out the word "hello" before Ike started telling him what had happened and that he was on his way to town as soon as he changed his tire. Joe told him that unless he needed medical attention, wait for him. He'd call in all his deputies and they'd meet to start a search.

Waiting around wasn't in Ike's wheelhouse, but there was little else he could do now, so he complied. After changing the tire, he checked the time. It felt like a half a day had passed instead of fifteen minutes.

With nothing to do but pace and stew over the situation, Ike started scouting around the area. He found tracks on the other side of the road and started following them, giving up a silent thanks to his father, who'd made him spend time with a tracker when he was a boy. Ike remembered his father telling him he never knew when those skills might save his life.

Right now, Ike hoped it was Rylee's life that would be saved. He couldn't figure who would want to hurt her, but now that his head was clearing, he felt that he'd seen the man who attacked them somewhere. The problem was, he just couldn't put his finger on where or when.

As he walked, searching the ground and the brush, it occurred to him he should call on Bear's father. Claude had tracking dogs and Ike knew how effective they could be. He pulled out his phone and made a call.

"Mr. Brickman, hello," Claude answered. "I've got two of my dogs in the truck, headed for your location. Matt, Tom, your dad, and the wranglers are gearing up now, trucks and horses. You'll have a team within half an hour."

"Thanks Claude, I'll be waiting."

Ike pocketed his phone and looked up at the sky. "You know I'm not much of a praying man, but I'm asking for your help now. Yeah, it's for me. The truth is, I don't know how I can face losing her. I understand you not feeling kindly enough toward me to grant my plea, but please don't forsake her. She's a good person, a kind one—someone who will give her life to save another. Please help us save her."

Ike didn't expect an answer or a sign, nor did he get one. All he had was his own determination to find and save her, if it was humanly possible. And if, in the end, he lost her to whoever had taken her, it'd be his life's mission to find and kill the man who took Rylee from him.

*****

Rylee woke with a start and immediately began fighting to free herself from being slung over the man's shoulder. She kicked, beat on his back, and screamed like a banshee, making him stumble. They both went tumbling, but she was the first on her feet and took off running back the way they'd come.

Unfortunately, she didn't get far before he tackled her. She landed hard; her face smacked into the dirt and stars swam before her eyes. When he grabbed her and yanked her up, she spit at him and saw blood in her sputum.

As crazy as it was, that summoned a memory from her childhood. When she was fourteen, she and her dad went camping in the North Carolina mountains and he taught her about finding things you could eat, how to determine what water source was safe and he told her about his family training trailing dogs.

She'd never heard the term and at first thought he was talking about the dogs police used to track people. He told her there was more to it than just shoving a dog's nose into a shirt or a footstep. He called it trailing theory.

It all came back to her in a flash. Trailing, her dad taught her, was training a dog to follow a particular human's scent pattern no matter where it was—on the ground or in the air. With this type of training, if the dog is following a scent trail on a path where the target is known to have walked, but then suddenly detects the same scene on the air coming from another direction, the animal is allowed to follow the air scent and deviate from the footpath.

It was her dad's opinion that trailing epitomized a canine's natural instincts to scent patterns and replicate what a wild canine, such as a wolf or coyote, would do when following prey based on scent. He taught her that every animal and human produces a distinctive order based upon species and other sub-determining factors like sex, age, and disease. The amount of odor produced also depends on primary factors such as mental condition, such as fear or anger, exertion, and relative health issues.

That memory brought a surge of hope. If Ike regained consciousness, and she had to believe he would, or she would lose it completely. But if he did, then he'd call for help. Thanks to Bear, she'd met his father, Claude, and been able to talk to him about the trailing dogs he trained. She knew, without doubt, that at some point he would put his dogs to work to find her.

And she was determined to help them. So, when her captor ordered her to turn and walk in front of him, she did, but every hundred steps she spit on the ground. By the time she saw the old black truck parked in scrubby trees, the man had noticed her spitting.

"What the hell you doing?"

"If I swallow this blood, I'll puke. You want me puking in your truck? Between that and my sinuses running like water thanks to all this–" she waved around them. "This stuff you people have growing in this wilderness, it's a wonder I don't drown in snot."

"Fine, spit all you want, but get in the damn truck."

She complied and rolled down her window. As soon as he started the engine, she sniffed as hard as she could and spit out of the window. With luck, she'd have enough blood and spit to mark a trail to wherever he was taking her.

Chapter Twenty-Six

Rylee had no clue where she was. Her mouth had gone dry at least fifteen minutes ago, so she bit her tongue hard enough to make it bleed and give herself something to spit. A few minutes later, the truck turned onto a rutted dirt part toward a dwelling that looked more of a shack than a home.

It hit her that she knew where they were. Ike told her about when his family rerouted a river that someone dammed to starve the Brickman's and others of much-needed water. Later, she rode the land with Matt and Tom, and they told her the story as well.

The man who once owned the property that cut between their property and others, attempted to dam the river, and cut off the water supply to four landowners and ranchers. Asa was still running things, and he rounded up the ranchers and had a meeting.

They took matters into their own hands. Brickman Ranch lay above the man's property, and with the river dammed, pastures to the north were flooding, while other ranches south of the man were drying up. So, Asa hired an excavation company, and they rerouted the river to bypass the man who was screwing them over. That's why the river now ran in a kind of strange crescent through Brickman land, and then over to Caldwell's place.

The man's son, a teenager, tried to kill Asa. Broke into his house and shot him. They gave him twenty years.

Rylee stole a glimpse at the man. No. This couldn't be the same man. If this was the same person, he wouldn't be this old. The man's face was so covered with beard it was hard to tell much about his looks. But the beard was gray, and he had age spots on his hands, so he had to be older than 50. And the teenage boy sent to prison was tried as an adult at 18. If he served the full 20 years, he'd be 38.

So, it couldn't be him. But someone wanted them to think it was.

Which brought up the question. Who was holding her hostage, and what was his goal?

The truck came to a stop, shuddered, clanked, and turned off. The man got out and circled around the front of the truck to open her door. "Get out."

She obeyed, and he took hold of her arm and jerked to get her moving toward the house. He kept hold of her arm as he unlocked the door, then shoved her through the doorway. She jerked to a stop, surprised when she looked at the interior.

It was obviously old, but clean and tidy. The fireplace boasted of a thick wooden mantel that appeared hand cut and polished. Two lanterns sat on the ends of the mantel, and in between was a series of photos framed in what also appeared to be hand-crafted frames. She wanted to get a closer look, but didn't want to anger the man with her curiosity.

"You see that chair?" he used his rifle to point to a heavy wooden chair across the room sitting beside the window.

"Yes."

"You sit there, and you don't get up lessen I tell you too. If you try to run or fight me, I'll nail your hands to the chair arms."

Rylee was not just frightened by his threat, but shocked at the easy way he issued the threat of brutality. "I won't give you any problems."

"You best not. Now sit."

She hurried to comply, and once seated, watched him lean his rifle beside the door, then load fresh wood into the fireplace. "Can I ask why you're doing this?"

He glanced at her and scowled. "Ain't your business."

"I don't understand why someone would kidnap a total stranger. There must be some reason, but I just can't make sense of it. Have we ever met?"

"No."

"So, this has nothing to do with me?"

"No."

"Then why? Do you hate the Brickman family?"

"No."

She fell silent, contemplating the situation. "Did you kill Donny Caldwell?"

"Yes."

"Why?"

"He was a threat."

"To you?"

"No."

"Then who?

"None of your business."

"I'm sorry, but this makes no sense at all. You don't seem like a man who'd kill indiscriminately, so if you killed someone, you'd have to have a reason, right?"

"Yes."

"And it wasn't because he wronged you?"

"No." He rose and crossed the room to the kitchen area, where he set about putting water and coffee into an old percolator pot.

She thought about it. There were a lot of reasons people committed awful crimes, and from what she'd read, some of those reasons made no sense because the perpetrators were mentally unbalanced.

"So, he did nothing at all to you?" she continued her questioning.

"Hush."

"Pardon?"

"Stop talking, or I'll sew your lips closed."

That shut her up and made a cold sweat seep from her pores. Maybe she should turn her mind to how she was going to escape, rather than trying to figure out his motives. It was clear he had no qualms about harming her. She needed to get away from him as quickly as possible.

Or get rescued. She said a silent prayer that Ike was alive and in no danger, and that he'd been found, cared for, and told someone what happened. Rylee might not have known Ike all that long, but one thing she was sure of was that he'd do everything he could to save her.

She just wished he would hurry.

*****

Ike waved the EMT away as soon as he affixed the bandage over the wound. Claude waited at Ike's truck with two of his dogs. Matt was in the back of Asa's truck, getting a drone ready to go into the air.

267

The plan was for Claude, Ike, Tom, and the dogs to take to the woods on horseback with several wranglers, while everyone else followed Matt and Asa. Tom and Ike would be in communication with Matt to let him know if the dogs picked up a scent, so that he could follow them based on the location of Ike's phone.

Claude had already walked the dogs around the area, and they found blood on the road that wasn't Ike's. That sent a spike of alarm through Ike. How badly was she injured? He almost hated to ask, but did query Claude, who assured him that the amount of blood they found didn't seem to show a serious injury. The EMT echoed his opinion.

Ike prayed the plan worked. He didn't want anyone to know how afraid he was that the man would harm Rylee. Heck, he was scared she'd provoke it by trying to escape.

"You okay, Dad?" Tom rode up beside Ike.

"Yeah, I'm fine, don't worry about me."

"We'll find her. The dogs have already picked up the scent. Send the location to Matt."

"On it." Ike pulled out his phone and texted Matt. "Stay above me. I'll keep behind the dogs. They've picked up the scent."

"We'll find her, Dad," Tom said.

Ike nodded. At present, he didn't want to talk. His mind was filling with visions of all the things that might happen to Rylee, and he had to find a way to push those images from his mind. The only way he knew to diminish the fear he felt for her was to turn it into anger, so he set his mind on what he'd do to the man if he hurt her. Ike lost track of time, lost in his own dark thoughts.

"They're on the run," Claude's announcement snapped him back to the present. "We must be close."

Ike's heart beat faster. If they didn't find Rylee alive and well, the man who hurt her was going to die. And God forgive him, but he'd made it slow and painful.

*****

At the cabin, Rylee was starting to fret. By her estimation, which she knew could be wrong, she guessed at least two hours had passed. It was getting close to dark. Would Ike be looking for her, and if so, would he use the dogs? If he did, would they pick up the scent?

Fear her hope was in vain was making her more scared for her life. Thus far, the man had not spoken to her, or offered her food or water. He simply sat at the small table in the kitchen, drinking coffee and staring at her.

When the sound of a phone shrilled, she jumped, terrified that the phone in her back pocket had rung. She quickly realized her mistake when her captor rose to go to the cupboard and pick up a cell phone. He turned his back on her when he answered, and she quickly reached to fish her own phone from her pocket.

One look and her hope of reaching out for help vanished. It was smashed all to hell. She shoved it under her leg just as the man turned. "She isn't doing anything. How long do I have to keep her here?"

He watched Rylee as he listened. "I don't want no more deaths on my head… yeah, I know, but she… yes, I know. Yes, I promised. Yes. Okay. I will."

When he put the phone on the table, he then walked to the door to fetch his rifle still propped against the wall. "Come on."

"Where?"

"Outside."

"Why?"

"Get up!"

When he started toward her, she jumped up. That made her phone clatter to the floor. The man roared and rushed her. "What have you done?" He clubbed her on the side of the head with his fist, knocking her to the floor. "Tell me! Who did you call?"

"No one!" she screamed and scooted back from him. "It's broken. Look for yourself!"

He snatched the phone off the floor, looked, and then hurled it at the fireplace. It smashed into the rock and shattered. Rylee scooted back from him like a crab as he advanced on her.

"Get up!"

"No," she continued to move back.

He leapt forward, took hold of her hair, and yanked her to her feet. Rylee screamed and fought him. At this point, it was the only thing she could do. Clearly, he'd been given orders to kill her and didn't want to do it inside.

Determined not to make it easy for him, she fought with every ounce of energy she possessed. Sadly, it wasn't enough. He rammed the stock of his rifle into her belly, driving the air from her and causing her to bend forward in pain. Then he clubbed her in the head.

Rylee saw double. Everything spun and swam, and she staggered, trying to stay upright. She thought she saw him lift the rifle to point it at her, and suddenly it sounded like the door was being rammed. It flew open and light flooded the dark cabin.

"If you want to draw another breath, you'll drop that weapon."

She heard Ike's voice, and all the energy fled her body. With a weak cry, she crumpled to the floor.

Chapter Twenty-Seven

"If he moves, shoot him," Ike ordered as he marched around the bearded man and squatted beside Rylee.

Tom and Claude drew their weapons and stepped up on either side of the man. Ike gently turned Rylee over onto her back and cupped her face with one hand. "Rylee? Can you hear me, sweetheart? Rylee?"

She blinked several times, looked up and him, and in one motion was off the floor and in his arms, clinging to him with all her might. "You came," she said, over and again. "You came."

When she suddenly went limp, Ike stood with her in his arms and looked at Tom. "Call for the helicopter. We need to get her to a hospital."

"On it."

Just then, Joe arrived with the wranglers and some of his own men. He took one look at the situation and assumed control. "Cuff him and put him in the back of my cruiser," he ordered two of his deputies, then glanced at the other two. "You search this place. We're looking for anything that connects him to the Caldwell boy's death, or Mark Windom's."

"Yes, sir," the deputies set to their tasks.

Ike marched past Joe to carry Rylee outside. He sat on the front step and patted her face. "Rylee, honey, you need to wake up. Can you hear me?"

She moaned and tried to bat his hand away. He tried again, but this time, when he touched her, her eyes flew open. She screamed and started fighting to get away. It took a few minutes to calm her down, but finally she ran out of steam and basically collapsed against his chest, sobbing. It killed him to see her this way. She was so full of life, so willing to love to feel compassion and put herself on the line for others.

Ike never wanted to fall in love with her, but damn if that isn't what happened, and seeing her suffer broke his heart.

Just then, he heard Matt's voice and looked up. The expression on Matt's face matched Ike's own feelings–concern and rage. "Dear God, Dad, what did he do to her?"

"I don't know. We'll find out once we get her to the hospital."

"Damn, it feels like we're one big unlucky charm for her. She keeps saving us, trying to help others, and all she gets for it is more pain. That doesn't seem right. All she wants is..."

When his voice trailed off, Ike looked up at him. "All she wants is what?"

"You. A home, a family, what we all want."

Ike nodded. "She's going to be fine. You hear me Rylee? You're going to be fine."

Tom stepped out of the house. "Joe's leaving two of his deputies until the state forensic team gets here. The chopper is ten minutes out. I'm headed back with the wranglers to where we left the horse trailers. I'll take your horse since I'm assuming you'll go to the hospital?"

"Yes."

"I'll get Pop and head on back to the ranch." Matt said, "Call when you have a report on her?"

"I will. Thank you." He looked from Matt to Tom. "Thank you both."

"No need for thanks," Tom replied, and Matt added, "Family takes care of family."

"Yes, sir," Ike agreed. "I'll talk to you soon."

Once everyone left except the deputies assigned to wait for the forensic team, Ike could let his guard down. He didn't care that tears gathered or spilled down his face. All he cared about was the woman in his arms, battered, bruised and bloody; the woman who was hurt because she loved him and all his family.

He wished now he'd killed the son-of-a-bitch, rather than let Joe take him to jail. But he knew Rylee would have been disappointed in him, and much to his surprise, that meant more than he ever imagined it could.

When he heard the chopper, he rose with her in his arms. Within minutes, he sat in the back, holding her as the bird lifted off.

Within twenty minutes, they were landing on the helipad on top of the hospital. Ike could see people waiting with a gurney. The moment the rotors stopped, the team of people hurried to the helicopter. Ike got out and placed her gently on the gurney, then followed as they wheeled her to the elevator.

Despite his insistence, they wouldn't let him in the emergency room. He went to the waiting room and found Liz and his mother there. They both hurried to him, and for a few moments, they all just held one another in a group hug. Then Georgia broke away and gestured toward a grouping of chairs. "Let's sit."

"What happened?" Liz asked as soon as they were seated.

"Someone shot out a tire, and then shot me and took Rylee."

"Shot you?" Georgia blurted, louder than normal.

"Just a flesh wound." He removed his hat, revealing the bandage. "And the man who took her looks so familiar, but I can't place him. I wish I could."

"It'll come to you," Georgia said. "How bad is Rylee hurt?"

"I don't know. She's beat all to hell."

"Oh God," Georgia put her hand to her chest, and Liz reached to take her hand. "Don't worry, GiGi, the doctors here are excellent. They'll take care of her." She then looked at Ike. "Should we call her brother?"

"Not until we have something to report."

The next two hours had to be among the longest in Ike's life. When the door opened and a doctor stepped in, they all jumped to their feet. "Are you the family of Rylee Monroe?"

"We are," Georgia spoke up. "How is she?"

"Lucky. She had to have some stitches in her head, has a cracked rib and a lot of bruises, but she'll be fine."

"Are you keeping her?" Ike asked.

"No, since she doesn't have a concussion and all her vitals are good, we'll let her go home. She's likely to be quite sore, so I'll send some pain medication with her. Just make sure she eats something before she takes it, and do your best to make her rest."

"We will," Ike promised.

"Excellent. You can wait with her while we fill out the discharge papers."

"Thank you."

Liz started to follow Ike, but Georgia took her arm. "Why don't we head on home and make sure there's a hot meal and warm bed ready for her?" Georgia looked at Ike. "You're taking the helicopter?"

"Damn, let me check if he's still there." Ike placed the call, which took only a few seconds. "Yeah, he's waiting. Be careful going home."

"We will." Liz gave Ike a kiss on the cheek and escorted Georgia out.

Ike hurried to the desk and asked where Rylee was. A nurse showed him to the room. The moment he walked in, she slid off the bed and ran to him. "Ouch!" She yelped as she wound her arms around his waist and hugged him tight.

"The doctor said you'll be fine."

"I'm much better now," she said against his chest, then looked up. "How are you standing? I know he shot you."

"Just a fresh wound. All bandaged up and good to go."

"You promise?"

"I do."

She hugged him tight again. "I was so scared I'd never see you again, that you'd lay on that road and–" Tears overwhelmed her, and she cried for a while as he held her.

"We're both fine and going to stay that way."

"Ike, that man did all this because someone told him to."

"How do you know that?"

"Because he got a phone call, and it sounded like whoever he was talking to was the one calling the shots. The police need to get that phone from his cabin."

"I'll let Joe know."

"And there are photos on the mantel—maybe of him, I don't know. They looked old, but maybe if–"

"Hey, slow down," he hushed her. "We'll tackle all this in the morning. For now, let's get you home, okay?"

"Okay, can we go now?"

"As soon as they bring your discharge papers. Do you mind if I call Joe while we wait?"

"No, of course not."

Ike made the call and put it on speaker. The first thing Joe said when he answered was, "How is she?"

"Banged up, but the doctor says she'll be fine."

"Thank God."

"What about the prisoner?"

"That's one tight-lipped SOB. He won't even give us his name. We'll take his prints and run them through the system to see if something pops. I can't search the county records to find out who owns that cabin until morning, so we all have to sit tight tonight.

"I'm going to need Rylee and you both to make statements. Can you come to the station tomorrow?"

"Yes," Rylee answered, and when Ike glanced at her added. "If it's okay with Ike."

He didn't see any need to argue. "If you're up to it in the morning, that'll be fine."

"Then I'll see you both tomorrow. Glad you're okay, Ms. Monroe."

"Thank you, Chief Rogers," she replied. "See you tomorrow."

Ike pocketed the phone and looked at her. "Don't feel like you have to push yourself. We can wait a day or two to let you rest and–"

"I'll be fine," she argued, and added in a softer tone. "Really, I will. I just need a shower and an hour-long soak in a hot tub and something to eat, and I'll be good to go."

"Uh huh," he didn't believe that for a moment, but wouldn't argue, since he was pretty sure she was trying her best to keep him from worrying about her.

Just then, a nurse arrived with a pill bottle and Rylee's discharge papers in a plastic bag. "Thank you," Rylee said as she accepted the bag. "I appreciate everything you did for me."

"You take care, Rylee."

"I will. Bye."

Ike escorted her to the elevator with roof access. When they stepped outside, Rylee stopped and looked up at the sky. "Would you look at that? Even the lights of the town can't defy their beauty." She then looked at him. "This is such a magnificent place. It's magical and spiritual, and romantic as well."

"Romantic?"

"Yes, the way the mountains kiss the sky. It's glorious."

"Indeed, it is. Come on, let's go home."

She nodded, and he saw the way her eyes filled with tears. Ike put his arm around her, and when they reached the helicopter, helped her inside. He buckled her in and then himself. For a few minutes, she watched the passing scenery, then she closed her eyes.

And within seconds was asleep.

Rylee didn't wake when they landed on the front lawn, or when Ike unfastened her and lifted her into his arms. He carried her inside, finding his entire family waiting.

"Is she okay?" Matt was the first to speak.

"Yeah, she'll be fine. But I'm going to put her to bed. It's been a hell of a day, and I think what she needs the most is rest."

"I can get her settled in," Georgia offered.

"No, I'll do it." Ike realized from the expression on everyone's face he'd shocked them, but he didn't care. He wasn't leaving Rylee alone until he was convinced she was okay, and secretly feared her physical injuries wouldn't be the worst of her suffering. He figured as soon as the initial shock wore off, she'd start having flashbacks to what happened, and that's when the mental suffering would begin.

And he'd be right there beside her, to make her feel safe.

Chapter Twenty-Eight

Twice during the night, she woke screaming, and each time Ike was there to hold her, driving the demons away with his calm voice, warm body, and soft touch. Rylee had experienced nothing like this since she was a child, feeling so surrounded by caring, so safe. It not only worked to quell her fears but also to make her fall even more in love with him.

The third time she woke, it was from pain. Ike got up to go into the bathroom and get her a glass of water and a pain pill. But when he came back into the bedroom, he stopped. "You're supposed to eat before taking this."

"Then I won't take it. Come back to bed."

"I can fix you—"

"Come back to bed."

She loved watching him walk over to the bed, wearing only his boxer briefs. Ike might not think he was anything special, but to her, he was perfect. As soon as he climbed into the bed, she snuggled close to him. "Thank you for rescuing me."

"Thank you for rescuing me."

She propped up on one elbow to look at him. "I didn't."

"Oh, you did."

"I did? From what?"

"Myself."

She didn't know what to make of that statement, so remained silent. After a moment, Ike spoke again. "When I woke on that road and you weren't there, it hit me. I could draw breath, my heart would continue to beat, but if something happened to you, I'd lose the best thing that ever happened to me."

"Really?"

"Really. I want to discover where this thing we have is going. Will you stay here with me while we figure it out?"

"I will."

"That's it? You don't want to lay down rules or get guarantees?"

"I just want you, Ike. Didn't you know that? If you decide it's not what you want, then I'll be broken, but I'll understand. I don't want someone who doesn't want me. But I sure would love to find out if this thing we have is something that can go the distance."

"So do I."

"Then we have a deal."

"Should we shake on it?"

"I think we can do better than that," she rolled over on top of him, and after that, there was no more need for words.

*****

The first thing he was aware of was the feel of her. She slept with her head on his shoulder, one arm on his chest with her hand on his neck, and a leg thrown over his. It hit him that he'd never awakened next to a woman, and it feel so right.

The age thing still nagged at him, but maybe she was right, and it didn't matter. God knew he wasn't a man to fall in love easily, but now that he had, perhaps it wasn't much of a sin to love a woman sixteen years his junior.

"Good morning," she raised her head to look at him.

"Good morning."

"I'm starving."

"Want me to get Bear to fix you a tray?"

"No. I want you to take a shower with me, and then go into the kitchen and sit at the bar and eat."

"I could use a shower."

"Then what are we waiting for?"

It was when she rolled off him and grunted that he chuckled. "You sure you want to get up?"

"Definitely," she slid off the bed. "Come on."

Ike wasn't expecting anything more than to get clean, but Rylee had other plans. As soon as they were wet, with the hot water showering down on them, she backed up against the shower wall and pulled him to her. The kiss turned into more, and before long, she had her legs around his waist, riding him with abandon.

By the time they were dressed and headed for the kitchen, he could hear voices. All three of his children sat at the bar, and all three looked at him when he and Rylee entered.

"I was starting to wonder," Tom said. "You never stay in bed this late."

"It was my fault," Rylee said and added. "Oh, and it feels worse than it looks."

Matt got up to hug her. "You look beautiful to me."

"Flatterer," she gave him a noisy kiss, then went to where Bear was taking biscuits out of the oven. "I'd kill for one of those."

"Have all you want."

Rylee snagged one and passed it back and forth from one hand to the other as it cooled. "Coffee?" Ike asked as he poured himself a cup.

"Yes, please, with lots of–"

"French vanilla creamer," he said, and went to the refrigerator to take the container from it.

"What a man," she said, and bit into the biscuit. "Oh my god, this is awesome."

"Sit," Ike commanded as he put her coffee on the bar.

She did, and after swallowing, asked. "I need a new phone. Can someone give me a ride to town? Also, I need to check in with work and–"

"Whoa, slow down," Ike said. "Let's have breakfast, and we'll figure it all out."

"Okay," she smiled and sampled the coffee. "Oh god, perfect."

"You want some eggs, Rylee?" Bear asked. "I have hash browns the way you like them, with chopped onion. And some country ham if you want some with another biscuit.

"Yes, please, to all of it," she smiled. "I swear you better be glad you're married, Bear, or I'd be after you like white on rice."

He grinned, and she turned her attention to the people at the bar. "So, I need to thank you all. You all saved me, and I want you to know that I won't ever forget it. I'm in your debt."

"No, you're not," Matt said.

"Family looks out for family," Tom added.

"And I did nothing to be thanked for," Liz said.

"Yes, you did. Ike told me you and Mrs. Georgia were at the hospital waiting with him. Thank you all." Rylee said. "You can't imagine what that means to me."

"Time to eat," Bear announced, and everyone's attention turned to food.

When they finished, Tom stood. "I need to get to it. Matt, are you working here today?"

"I am. Let's do it."

"I'll walk with you," Liz said.

"I need to head down and check with Claude," Ike said to Rylee. "Want to walk with me?"

"No, if it's okay, I think I'll stay here and help Bear clean up and have another coffee."

"Okay, I'll be back in an hour."

"Take your time." She gave him a quick kiss, then turned her attention to scraping off plates and taking them to the sink. Rylee hated to admit how sore she was. She felt every muscle and knew that if she didn't keep moving, she'd stiffen up and it would hurt even worse.

It surprised her how quickly the time passed. Bear was comfortable to be around, and she liked him. When he asked about learning about programming, she offered to work with him and decided she'd surprise him with some textbooks and a laptop. That way, he could study when he had free time. Rylee couldn't wait to get on her own laptop and order everything for him, but reminded herself that maybe she should consult Ann to make sure it wouldn't cause any issues.

"Penny for your thoughts," Ike's voice had her turning from where she stood at the counter, wiping down the countertops.

"Sorry, they're worth at least a nickel." She smiled at him.

"You ready to head to town?"

"I am."

"Then grab your gear and let's get to it."

"Yes, sir!" She hurried to put everything she thought she'd need into her messenger bag, and found him parked out front in his truck with the passenger door open.

She got in and he started down the drive. "Tell me what's happening on the ranch," she said. "Did you decide to sell that Hot Smoke, or just keep him to breed?"

"I reckon we'll keep him for a while longer."

"I bet it's hard to let one go after you've put so much time and love into training them."

"What makes you think I love them?"

"It's on your face when you look at them or ride them. You're not nearly as hard to read as you think."

"No?"

"Well, you were at first, but now I'm starting to recognize your expressions and what you do with your eyes."

"What I do with my eyes?"

"Yes, I remember reading a book once about how people's eyes give them away."

"I don't think that applies to me."

"But it does. When someone says something that annoys you, at first your eyes narrow ever so minutely, then you lower your head just a bit, and press your lips together a little before you speak. When you hear something that pleases you, often you blink and reach up to rub your philtrum–"

"My what?" he interrupted.

"Philtrum," she stoked her index finger over the small indentation above her lip. "Or medial cleft. It's this little vertical indentation. Anyway, you do that, then you smile."

"You're very observant, aren't you, Rylee Monroe?"

"How long will you keep calling me Rylee Monroe?"

"Does it bother you?"

"No, it's just—different."

"Is your real name Rylee?"

"Sort of. It's Ryanna Lee Monroe, but I've always gone by Rylee."

"It's beautiful. Unusual. Is it a family name?"

"Sort of. My dad's name was Ryan, and my mom's name was Anna. Anna Lee. So, they named me after both."

"That's something to be proud of."

"They were people to be proud of. You would have liked them."

"I already do."

She smiled at his kindness. "That's sweet, but you don't know them."

"Sure, I do. They're inside you."

That shocked and touched her, and she quickly swiped at her eyes as he continued. "They'll be part of you as long as you live, sweetheart, and if you have children, they and you will be part of them. That's how we keep our immortality."

Rylee reached over to give his arm a squeeze. "I love you, Ike Brickman."

As soon as the words were out, she tensed and gazed out of the window, sure she'd overstepped and screwed things up.

"You sure make it impossible for a man not to love you, Ryanna Lee Monroe."

It wasn't a declaration–at least not an overt one, but it was enough. And he'd given her the ammunition to turn it into something less serious, so she took it. "Ryanna Lee Monroe, eh? That's a mouthful for everyday use, don't you think?"

"I do, but I plan on using it, anyway."

"Fine," she agreed. "So, tell me all about your horses."

"You really want to hear me go on about that?"

"I do. I'm interested in what you do and how you became the best. So, talk to me, Ike Brickman."

He smiled, and after a few seconds, started talking. Rylee loved to listen to him speak, and she could hear in his voice how much he loved what he did. She asked questions, as was her habit, and the conversation lasted throughout the drive into town.

"First stop, phone store?" He asked as they reached the city limits.

"Yes please."

It took her ten minutes thanks to there being no other customers in the store, and that she knew exactly what she wanted. Rylee declined the clerk's offer to set up her phone and restore her data from the Cloud, thanked the young woman and left.

"Now No Limits," she said to Ike as she got back into the truck.

The moment they walked in, Lynda yelled "Rylee's here!" In seconds, all the employees were flooding into the reception area.

"What's going on?" Rylee asked.

Jack answered. "I was getting ready to–oh my God, what happened to you?"

"I'll tell you later. Finish what you were saying."

"Oh, okay, I was about to set the system for a full backup when I discovered one server contained an encrypted file."

"What was on it?" she asked.

"I have no clue. I can't break in."

"Seriously?"

"Yes."

She looked at Ike. "I think it's time for Ryanna Lee Monroe to give it a go."

"Ryanna, what?" Kyle asked.

"Never mind," Rylee said over her shoulder. "Ike, you coming?"

"After you."

She headed for the control room, with Ike and Jack behind her. "Show me," she said when she sat down in front of one of the Macs.

Jack sat beside her, and she slid the keyboard to him. He located the file and slid the keyboard back to her.

Rylee stared at the screen for a moment before she attempted to access the file. When she received an error, she pushed back a bit and stared some more. "This will take some time," she announced.

"You know what that nonsensical error means?" Jack asked.

"Indeed, I do. The question is, can I break it before it self-destructs."

"As in blows up?" Ike asked.

"In a manner of speaking, if you have something else to do, I don't mind. Like I said, this will take some time."

"Nope, I'll stay."

"Then pull up a chair."

He did, and when he slid it beside her, she leaned over and gave him a kiss. "For luck."

Ike grinned and Rylee turned her attention to the battle at hand.

Chapter Twenty-Nine

Ike was starting to feel like he had a vat of acid in his gut. They're arrived at No Limits at a quarter past nine and Rylee had been clickity-clacking on the keyboard for six straight hours while he and Jack watched, drank vats of coffee, and competed for who had to make the most trips to the bathroom.

He'd never seen anyone with such concentration. Rylee didn't seem to be aware of their presence. Her entire focus was on the monitor. When she suddenly blurted, "Got'cha!" it almost startled him.

"What?" Jack asked.

"See for yourself." She clicked on the now available mp4 file, and a video player window opened. "That's the same footage as before," Ike said as the video of Donny Caldwell getting hit, played."

"But that isn't," she said.

Sure enough, this footage was different. It appeared to be one of the park and showed a black truck parking along the sidewalk entrance. A man got out and hurried to another car parked nearby, this one with its back tires to the sidewalk and the front of the car facing the direction of the camera that was taping the scene.

"Holy hell, that's Sharon Dellinger's car," Ike announced.

"And the man who kidnapped me," Rylee added.

"And who's that?" Jack pointed to another car parked behind the truck in the parking lot rather than the curb.

"Somebody's screwing. Surely the woman in the car has to see them."

As they watched, the passenger door of Mark's car opened, and a woman got out. She appeared to be in her early to mid-thirties. "I know her," Jack said. "She works at the grocery store."

"Look!" Rylee pointed.

Mark and the mayor clearly saw one another when he pulled out to leave, because they looked directly at one another.

"Shit on a stick," Ike grumbled, removed his hat, ran his hand through his hair and then leaned back, blew out a breath and stared at the ceiling.

"I don't get it," Jack admitted.

"Rylee, can you copy that?" Ike ignored Jack's question. "We need to take it to Joe. Now."

"Of course." She got up to get a memory card and quickly made a copy, then addressed Jack. "Don't let anyone touch this. We're going to leave this room and lock the door behind us. Then you're going to tell everyone to take the day off and you all are going to lock up and leave."

"Don't you think—"

"Jack, just do it. Never mind. I will. Come on."

Once they were out of the room, she set the lock, then went into the reception area, calling out as she did. "Hey, I need to see you all. Now."

It didn't take long for everyone to assemble, and as soon as they did, she addressed them. "You're all getting the rest of the day off, so grab your stuff and go. I'll lock up. No one comes back inside this office until you hear from me. Got it?"

"Can I ask–" Sheila was saying when Rylee cut her off.

"No, sorry. No questions. I'll explain when I can. Now go. Enjoy your day. I'll be in touch."

Once everyone left, she looked at Ike. "This is looking much worse, you know that, right?"

"I do."

"And she's your friend."

"So, I thought. Maybe I was wrong."

"Then you want Joe to see this?"

"It's the right thing to do."

"That's my guy," she said and hugged him tight for a moment. "Okay, let's lock up and go."

Ike called Joe as they got into Ike's truck. The conversation was brief and when he finished, he looked at Rylee. "He's waiting for us."

Sure enough, the moment they walked into the police department, one of the deputies told them to go on back to the chief's office.

"Talk to me," Joe said when they walked in.

"Best you see it for yourself," Ike answered.

"May I put this memory card into your computer?" Rylee asked.

"Have at it," Joe agreed.

She plugged in the card and started the video. Within moments, Joe was scooting up closer. "Jesus," he breathed and when the video ended looked from Rylee to Ike. "You know what this looks like?"

"Like the Mayor's involved in the deaths," Rylee said. "The man who got into her car ran down Donny. The same man who shot Ike and kidnapped me. The same man sitting in your jail. Now, considering that Mark saw him with the mayor, it leads us to hypothesize that he is likely to be responsible for Mark's death as well, and thanks to the footage provided by Matt, Brent as well."

"Son of a–" Joe pushed back, stood, and went to his office door. "Curtis, bring that prisoner to my office."

As they waited, Rylee thought about it and suddenly something clicked into place. "Those photos on the mantel of his house. The ones of him and the blonde girl?"

"What about them?" Joe asked.

"Did the investigators take photos?"

"Yeah."

"Do you have them?"

"They're on my computer."

"Can you call them up?"

"Fine." Joe rapped on the keyboard. "Okay, here they are."

Rylee hurried to stand beside Joe. "Ike? Look."

He did, and then looked at her. "And?"

"Look closer. Both of you. Who's that girl?"

Suddenly Joe blurted. "Son of a bitch, that's Sharon. Sharon and that strange fellow, Marvin West. Remember him, Ike? He worked on Sharon's family's ranch. There was some gossip when she was in high school about her sleeping with the hired help. We all figured her daddy would fire Marvin, but he kept him on."

The door to the office opened, and a deputy escorted the bearded man inside. "Hello, Marvin," Joe greeted him.

The man stopped, looked down at the floor, blew out a breath and then looked at Joe. "Hey, Joe."

"So, it is you." Ike said. "You're the one responsible for all this meanness? What the hell happened to you, Marv? You were always a decent man, as far as I knew. What in hell would make you go and do something like this?"

"Love," Marvin said simply.

"Oh god," Rylee whispered. "Love? What kind of screwed up love makes a man run down a teenage boy?"

"I reckon the kind you can't understand."

"Then sit and explain it to us," Ike said and gestured to a chair.

That's exactly what Marvin did, and when he was finished and a deputy had escorted him back to his cell, Joe looked at Ike and Rylee. "This is going to be one hell of a shitshow, you know that, right?"

"I do."

"Did you record him?" Rylee asked.

Joe pointed to the microphone in the penholder on his desk. "Clever," she said.

"I'll have it written up and ask him to read and sign it," Joe told them. "And then we'll move to the next step."

"Arresting Sharon, you mean?" Ike asked.

"Yep."

Ike nodded. "Then we'll get out of your hair unless there's something you need from us?"

"No, you've done enough. Go on home."

They left and neither of them spoke until they were in the truck headed home. "You did it," Ike said softly.

"Did what?"

"Solved the mystery, uncovered the guilty party and with luck, secured justice for all the people who've died."

"Funny, but I'm not feeling all that proud or pleased."

"It's a dirty business, lying and killing, ruining people's lives to save face or power. Makes me ashamed that I was too damn dense to see her for who she is."

Rather than try to find words when none would make a difference, Rylee just reached for his hand and gave it a squeeze. When they arrived at the ranch, Rylee felt like a month had passed and was suddenly exhausted.

"I feel dirty. I think I'll go in and get clean and maybe rest a while."

"Mind some company?"

"I was hoping you'd ask.

They'd only stepped inside when Ike grabbed her and shoved her behind him. "If you've hurt any-"

"No one was here when I arrive," Sharon said and waved the gun in her hand in the direction of the family room. "Let's go have a chat, shall we?"

Ike kept himself between Sharon and Rylee as they went into the family room. He sat on the sofa and Rylee perched beside him. Sharon stood in front of them, holding the gun.

"Marvin told us everything," Ike said to her.

"Everything what? You think you can believe a word that comes out of that old fool's mouth?"

"I did," Rylee answered, despite the look Ike gave. "He's been in love with you since you were a teenager. But you already know that, don't you?

"He'd do anything for you. That's why he killed Donny. He told us that Donny did landscaping work for you and one day while he was working on trimming your bushes, he went into your laundry room to get some water and he heard you talking to someone, so he snuck in to eavesdrop and saw you with Brent. You had your backs to the door, but he could see what you were watching on the laptop on the kitchen counter.

"It was a video from your brother's restaurant. Earl and your sister-in-law were having sex in the office. And there was one of him and her right here in your house. You told Brent that thanks to the cameras he installed for you, you had enough to force Earl out of your life, have your brother kick his cheating wife to the street, you'd take everything you and Earl owned and he'd be left penniless. And you warned Brent to keep his mouth shut."

Rylee could see the rage simmering and wondered how much Sharon would take before she lost control. It might be wise to stop now, but Rylee wasn't in the mood to cower again. She was sick of being shot and beaten and terrorized. So, she continued.

"You never knew, but Marvin did. He caught Donny coming back into the laundry room. Donny swore he was just getting water, but Marvin didn't believe him, and neither did you when Marvin told you.

"So, when you ordered Marvin to get rid of Donny, he did what you asked. He always did what you asked. He'd loved you since you were fifteen and didn't know how to stop loving you. So, he killed Donny. Only Mark Windom saw it happen. And instead of reporting it, he tried to blackmail you.

"And you couldn't have that, so you had Marvin kill him as well, and Brent. Then he tried to kill Matt and Ike and me, but he failed."

"It's a good thing you're not a writer. You'd be a miserable failure and be laughed out of the business. Your story's full of holes. Your evil villain had no reason to kill Brent and Matt, Ike or you."

"It would seem that way, wouldn't it? And that's what you wanted. You had him kill Brent because you feared Brent had a copy of the videos and could testify against you. And you had him go after Matt and me because it made it seem like it had something to do with the old grudge, since Ike, Mark and Caldwell were involved in the river rerouting. In short, it cast suspicion in another direction."

"But you didn't count on Rylee," Ike joined the conversation.

"Fuck you, Brick," Sharon barked and waved the gun. "You and this bitch couldn't mind your own business, could you?"

"Our own business?" Rylee chimed in. "How dare you? If I remember correctly, you were one of the people begging me to get to the bottom of things and help find Donny's murderer. And all the while, you ordered his death."

"Oh, Miss high and fucking mighty, aren't you? Showing up and five minutes later jumping in bed with a man old enough to be your father."

Rylee laughed. "Not even, but whatever. This isn't about me or Ike. It's about you. You may not have driven the vehicle or pulled the trigger, but you're as guilty as Marvin for the deaths and you'll answer for those crimes."

"Not going to happen, you smug bitch!" Sharon pointed the gun at Ike. "Let's see how smug you are when his brains are decorating the wall." She fired, and the shot caught Ike in the upper left chest and spun him around.

That washed away any fear that remained, holding Rylee rooted in place. She'd not let Ike die. With a scream, she dove at Sharon. The impact when she hit Sharon sent them both stumbling. Sharon tripped and went down, and Rylee on top of her. Being heavier and bigger, Sharon had the advantage, pushed Rylee off and scrambled to her feet.

Rylee jumped up and rushed at Sharon, but Sharon pulled the trigger and the shot caught Rylee in the side and sent her careening backwards, reaching for purchase. She banged into the wall, feeling for something to hold on to. Her hand closed on the fire iron and as Sharon took aim again, Rylee pushed away from the wall and swung the iron.

The hooked end caught Sharon in the eye. She staggered, uttered a grunt, and then collapsed. Rylee hobbled over to where Ike had gotten to his feet and was holding his arm, headed for her.

"Ike," she managed to say before she felt it coming, a darkness that seemed intent upon swallowing her. "Ike."

Ike caught her as she collapsed and sank to the floor, holding her. He fished his phone from his shirt pocket and dialed 911. "This is Ike Brickman. I need an ambulance at my ranch. There's been a shooting."

He dropped the phone and gathered Rylee up more snuggly against him. "Rylee, wake up." He pleaded and shook her. She didn't respond. Her body just hung limply.

"No," he pleaded. "No, please no. Rylee wake up.

Time lost all meaning. There was only this moment, her in his arms and him begging her and God for her to stay with him. *Please,* he begged. *If you have to take her, then take me, too.* In this time of pain, he fully realized what she meant to him and knew he didn't want to live in a world where she did not exist.

He blinked, wondering why the light was dimming, and then realized the darkness held the answer to his plea and he surrendered to it, filled at last with the kind of love he thought he'd never have.

Chapter Thirty

Ike woke at the touch of a warm hand on his shoulder, shaking him. He looked up at his son, Matt. "I want you to come with me."

"Not much in the mood, son." That wasn't a lie. He hadn't been in the mood for much over the last three months. He'd survived the gunshot and so had Rylee, in a fashion. She'd survived two surgeries but was so weakened, the doctors put her into an induced coma to save her.

He'd spent nearly every day at the hospital, sitting by her bed, talking, or reading to her. The only time he left was to go home, shower, and change clothes. He ate in the hospital cafeteria and spent half an hour after lunch, sitting outside on a bench, watching the sky, and praying for a miracle.

That was where Matt had found him and now stood looking down at him. "Come on, Dad." Matt pleaded.

"Fine." Ike got to his feet and followed Matt inside.

He didn't question why Matt led him to Rylee's room. He was too full of fear, afraid he'd walk into that room to face losing her again. This time permanently.

But he wouldn't show that weakness to his son, so when Matt opened the door and gestured for Ike to precede him, Ike entered the room.

Astonishment had him freezing in place. Rylee sat up in bed, pale and thin but awake and smiling at him. *Thank you.*

Ike now knew what genuine gratitude felt like, because he felt it through every cell in his body.

"Hey there, handsome," she said in a voice that was gravely and weak.

"Rylee." He covered the rest of the distance in four steps, sat on the bed and took her into his arms, holding her firmly but gently. "You're okay?"

"I am," she replied.

"God in heaven, I thought I was going to lose you." He lowered her gently back onto the pillow.

"Do you think for one moment I'd willingly leave you?" She smiled up at him, reaching for his hand and then lifting it to her lips. "Sharon?"

"Dead."

"Am I going to go to prison for murdering her?"

"It was self-defense. No charges will be filed. And it wasn't murder. It was self-defense. You were trying to survive. And you saved my life."

"I still killed her. Do you think God will forgive me for that?"

"I am certain of it."

She nodded and stared into his eyes for a few moments. "I heard you."

"Heard me?"

"Talking to me. Humming and holding my hand, telling me about the ranch and the family. I heard you. It seemed like it was from a long way off. I wanted to tell you I was here, but nothing worked."

Her eyes filled with tears, and he cupped her face, brushing them away with his thumbs. "You're here and you're okay." He turned to look at Matt, who stood beside the door. "Right?"

"Yes sir. The doctor said she's a miracle."

"That she is," Ike agreed, and turned his attention to Rylee. "You've gotta quit getting yourself shot, sweetheart, or you're going to give me a heart attack."

"I told you Wyoming had it in for me."

He chuckled. "Well, I'll let the state in on a little secret, it doesn't stand a chance against you. You're the most courageous person I've ever known, and I don't think anything can beat you."

"There's always something bigger, stronger, faster or smarter than yourself," she argued. "But I'm through looking for answers, trying to solve the mysteries. All that's behind me."

"Oh? So, what's next, Ryanna Lee Monroe?"

"Well, I was thinking I'd propose to you."

"Pardon?"

"I'm asking you to be mine, Ike. Be mine and let me be yours."

Ike felt the man he once was just abruptly sloughed off like a snake shedding old useless skin. The man who didn't believe in love and happily ever after was gone. This girl who never backed down, surrendered, or gave up hope had peeled away all those useless layers and revealed what lay hidden.

A man in love. For the first time, truly in love.

"Well?" she asked.

"Well, I think that's a fine idea, with one provision."

"Which is?"

"That we make it official. Marry me?"

"Name the day, handsome."

Ike took her into his arms. This wasn't how he thought his life would go, but damn if he wasn't pleased. Sometimes life delivers you blessings you never realized you wanted, and when it does, you grab hold and don't let go.

That's exactly what he intended to do.

The End

A closing note:

I've been a reader my entire life, finding solace, excitement, happiness, fear and love in the pages of books. If anything has been a constant in my life, it's reading.

I also remember all the times in my life when being able to buy a book was a luxury, a treat that I didn't get every week. I've never forgotten those times or how much those books meant to me.

That's why I am so grateful to you, the readers. Regardless of your level of income or profession, I understand how precious your reading dollars are and I feel humbled that you've used some of those dollars to purchase my books.

I hope my stories prove worthy of your investment and thank you from the bottom of my heart.

Many blessings.

CPSIA information can be obtained
at www.ICGtesting.com
Printed in the USA
BVHW061956281221
625048BV00017B/2169/J

9 780998 580883